He was a lawman.

He faced dangerous people with guns and knives and every sort of weapon they could get their hands on. But none of them had shaken him the way that this woman did... He desperately wanted to put his hands on her arms or shoulders—anywhere, so long as he was touching her.

"What are you thinking?" he asked quietly.

The nearness of his voice surprised her...

She whirled around and backed her hands behind her on the edge of the sink. She wanted, no, *needed*, for the meal to be over and for Deputy Daniel Redwing to be gone. Otherwise she would be unable to keep her eyes from straying to his lips, her senses from remembering every reckless second she'd spent in his arms...and her heart from wishing that things could be different.

Available in July 2006 from Silhouette Special Edition

For the Love of Pete
by Sherryl Woods
(Summer Affairs)

The Hero Returns
by Joan Elliott Pickart
(Most Likely To…)

Redwing's Lady
by Stella Bagwell
(Men of the West)

Prescription: Love
by Pamela Toth
(Montana)

The Other Side of Paradise
by Laurie Paige
(Seven Devils)

Family Merger
by Leigh Greenwood

Redwing's Lady

STELLA BAGWELL

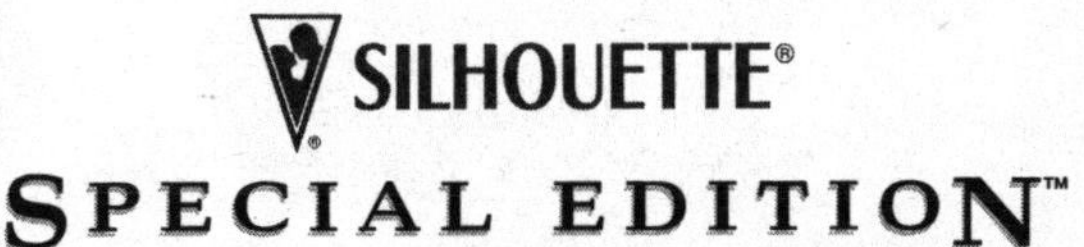

All the characters in this book have no existence outside the imagination of the author, and have no relation whatsoever to anyone bearing the same name or names. They are not even distantly inspired by any individual known or unknown to the author, and all the incidents are pure invention.

First published in Great Britain 2006
Silhouette Books, Eton House, 18-24 Paradise Road, Richmond, Surrey TW9 1SR

Standard ISBN 0 373 24695 1
Promotional ISBN 0 373 60443 2

23-0706

Printed and bound in Spain
by Litografia Rosés S.A., Barcelona

STELLA BAGWELL

sold her first book to Silhouette in November 1985. More than fifty novels later, she still loves her job and says she isn't completely content unless she's writing. Recently, she and her husband of thirty years moved from the hills of Oklahoma to Seadrift, Texas, a sleepy little fishing town located on the coastal bend. Stella says the water, the tropical climate and the seabirds make it a lovely place to let her imagination soar and to put the stories in her head down on paper.

She and her husband have one son, Jason, who lives and teaches maths in nearby Port Lavaca.

To my dear sister-in-law, Dorothy Sutmiller.
Love you!

UTE LEGEND OF THE BEAR DANCE

The origin of the Bear Dance can be traced back to the fifteenth century, when the Spaniards first came upon the Utes in springtime. As the Ute legend goes, two brothers were out hunting. When they became tired and lay down to rest, one of the men noticed a bear standing upright and facing a tree. The animal was dancing and making a noise while clawing the tree. The one brother ignored the animal and went on hunting, while the other brother continued to be mesmerised by the bear. The bear taught the young man the song he was singing and the dance that went with it. He told the young man to return to his people and teach them the dance and the songs of the bear. The songs would show respect for the spirit of the bear and that respect would make his people strong.

Each spring, the Bear Dance allowed the Ute people to release their tensions. After the fourth day of great celebrating, the men and women would leave a plume on a cedar tree, which meant they could leave their troubles behind and start life anew.

Chapter One

Deputy Daniel Redwing skidded to a stop in front of the rambling log ranch house and jumped from the pickup truck. Red dust continued to boil up from the tires, settling on his black Stetson and the khaki shirt stretched across his broad shoulders. It was late spring in northern New Mexico and already the high desert was thirsting for rain.

Maggie Ketchum was fumbling wildly with the latch of her yard gate. As he strode quickly in her direction, he noticed how the hot afternoon breeze was blowing bright red strands of her hair into her face.

He was halfway there when she finally managed to fling open the gate and rush toward him. She looked terror stricken as she exclaimed, "Deputy Redwing! What are *you* doing here?"

Daniel stopped short. Maybe the call had been a hoax, he thought hopefully. This was one time he wished like hell it had been. "Didn't you telephone the sheriff's office for help?"

Swiping a hand at her tangled hair, she nodded vigorously. "Yes! But I thought Jess was coming. I specifically asked for him!"

Daniel flared his nostrils slightly, but that was the only outward emotion he displayed at her comment. Jess Hastings was Maggie's brother-in-law and a damn good undersheriff for San Juan County. But Daniel wasn't inept. Or maybe she hadn't meant to imply that at all. He tried to be fair. The woman was obviously stressed to the point of breaking. Having her brother-in-law with her at a time like this would be more of a comfort than the chief deputy of the San Juan County Sheriff's Department.

"Sorry," he told her. "I figured you knew Jess was out of town. He and Sheriff Perez are down in Santa Fe at an emergency management meeting." He stepped closer. "The dispatcher said your call had something to do with Aaron missing. Have you found him yet?"

Aaron was Maggie's nine-year-old son and the only child she'd had with Hugh Ketchum before he'd been killed in a ranching accident with a bull. This woman had already been through one tragedy in her young life. Daniel couldn't imagine her going through two.

"No!" she wailed, then lowering her head, she pressed a hand over her eyes and muttered, "Oh God, Daniel, I don't know what to do! I've looked everywhere—the ranch hands are scouring the mesa, but they haven't found him!"

A sob stuck in her throat, but she choked it back and lifted her head to look at him with pleading blue eyes. At that moment Daniel wanted to step forward and pull her into his arms. But then, that was something he'd wanted to do with the Ketchum widow for months now—ever since he'd come to the T Bar K to investigate Noah Rider's murder.

For several years now, he'd known of Maggie Ketchum. Every now and then he would spot Hugh's pretty widow in town, going about the business of shopping and running errands. She was a member of the rich Ketchum family, a family that had settled in San Juan County more than sixty years ago and established the T Bar K Ranch, a range of property that took up a big hunk of northern New Mexico. Three sons and one daughter had been born to Tucker and Amelia Ketchum: Hugh, Seth, Ross and Victoria. Only the last three members of the family were living, and they co-owned the ranch, along with Maggie, who had inherited Hugh's share after his untimely death.

Daniel had never expected to meet Maggie face-to-face. She was hardly the type of woman who moved in a county deputy's social circle. But almost a year ago, the remains of Noah Rider, a one-time foreman of the T Bar K, had been discovered on the Ketchum property. As a result, Daniel had been handed the job of interviewing some of the family members who lived on the ranch. Maggie had been one of them. And he hadn't been able to forget her since.

"Calm down, Maggie. We'll find him. But first I need to ask you a few things. Let's go to the porch—out of the sun," he suggested.

She nodded jerkily, and he took her by the upper arm and led her through the wooden gate and across a small yard kept green by sprinklers. One end of the elevated porch was shaded by a ponderosa pine. Daniel guided her to the cooler shadows where rattan furniture was grouped in a cozy circle.

After helping her into one of the chairs, he took a seat to her right and eased his Stetson off his head.

Watching his slow, purposeful movements caused Maggie to erupt with impatience. "We're wasting time sitting here like this!" she argued. "We need to be out looking! And I still would have been searching if I hadn't taken the time to come here to the house to call the sheriff's department!"

Seeing she was on the verge of becoming hysterical, Daniel reached for her hand and gripped it tightly. "Look, Maggie, it doesn't do any good to run about searching here and there without any sort of direction or reason."

She stared at him with wild blue eyes. "That's easy for you to say! You don't have a child! You don't know what it's like to think he might—"

"Stop it, Maggie!" he interrupted roughly. "If you want to find Aaron you've got to get a grip on yourself and help me. Do you understand?"

His sternness seemed to get through to her, and her shoulders sagged as she nodded dutifully. "Yes. I'm sorry, Deputy Redwing. It's just that I'm so worried and—"

He squeezed her hand. "You called me Daniel a minute ago," he said gently. "Why don't you keep it that way? And there would be something wrong with you if you weren't worried. So now that we understand each other, tell me when Aaron went missing."

She drew in a deep, shuddering breath, then released it. "I don't know."

"Okay," he said, then started over again. "When was the last time you saw your son?"

"About eleven-thirty. He finished his lunch and then asked me if he could go down to the ranch yard to visit with Skinny. I gave him permission and told him to be back home by one."

Skinny was the oldest ranch hand on the T Bar K. Somewhere in his seventies, the man had worked for the Ketchum family for as long as he and everyone else on the ranch could remember. The old cowboy was good at telling tall tales, and all the kids loved him. Daniel figured it wasn't unusual for Aaron to go for a daily visit with Skinny.

Glancing at his wristwatch, he noticed it was nearly three. "Does Skinny know when Aaron left the ranch yard?"

She shook her head. "He says that Aaron never showed up. So I can only assume that for some reason or other he never went there."

The T Bar K Ranch was an enormous property of more than a hundred thousand acres with the ranch house and working headquarters nestled among the foothills of the San Juan Mountains. The nearest neighbors lived miles away, and since none of them had children, Daniel doubted very much that Aaron had headed to any one of the bordering properties, but there was always a remote chance.

"Do you think someone might have picked him up…and…and kidnapped him?" Maggie stammered out the fearful thought that had been going around in her head all afternoon.

No doubt about it, the Ketchums were a rich family, Daniel thought. They'd be able to pay a huge ransom to get one of their own back into the family fold. But Daniel didn't believe any such evil thing had happened, and he quickly shook his head to allay Maggie's fears.

"No. The only strangers who come here on the ranch are cattle or horse buyers—not perverts out to kidnap a little boy."

She gripped his hand and leaned toward him as though she needed to be closer to make him understand her fears. Daniel could have told her he was already feeling her pain. It radiated from her eyes and emanated from the rigid lines of her body.

"But how can you be so sure? Noah Rider was

murdered on this place, and nobody knew it for a long time! And even then—"

"Maggie!" he gently scolded. "Forget about all that. It's in the past. Noah was killed by an old acquaintance—Rube Dawson. He was a blackmailer who didn't want to lose his illicit income. Rube's serving his time in prison, and that crime has nothing to do with Aaron. Now tell me, were you and your son getting along all right at lunchtime? Was he angry at you about anything in the past few days?"

Going still, she looked him directly in the eye. "You think he's run away."

Daniel nodded, and as soon as he did, he could see tears flood her blue eyes. The sight cut him right through the heart.

"Maybe."

She looked away from him and swallowed hard. "Aaron didn't seem to be upset at lunch," she said in a strained voice. "He seemed fine. But he was angry with me yesterday. I wouldn't allow him to go on a weekend camping trip with a group of boys."

"Why?"

She frowned. "What does that have to do with anything? It won't tell us where Aaron is."

"Maybe. Maybe not," he said smoothly. "Right now I need every bit of information to go on. And I mean everything," he repeated firmly.

Once again she breathed deeply and tried to brace herself against the swell of terror washing over her. "All right. I didn't allow Aaron to go because the trip was going to be with a group of teenagers. And since Aaron is only nine, I didn't really want him to be exposed to the language and behavior that would be going on behind the chaperones' backs."

"He's got to hear it sometime."

Maggie grimaced. "Yes. But I'd rather it be later. So I told him he couldn't go and to forget about it. Of course he came back with the usual things that kids say when they're angry. That I was mean to him. That I didn't want him to have any fun. That I wouldn't let him do anything because I—"

She suddenly stopped, and her eyes fell to their coupled hands. Daniel wondered if she was noticing the stark difference between their skins. His, dark copper-brown; hers, milk-white. Daniel was a Ute Indian, from the Weeminuche band, something he didn't much think about—until he was with this woman.

"Because you what?" he prodded.

Her head shook slightly back and forth. "Because I was too scared—that I was afraid he would be killed in an accident—like his father."

Whether that was true or not didn't matter at the moment, Daniel decided. Aaron obviously believed his mother was overprotective, and he figured the boy had lashed out at her by disappearing.

"We'll find him, Maggie." Rising from the chair, he helped her to her feet. "Did you see him when he left the house to go down to the ranch yard?"

"No. I heard the back door slam. I didn't bother to look. I was busy in the kitchen."

Daniel frowned. "You say the back door? If he were going to walk down the road to the ranch yard, the front door would have made more sense. Would you take me around to the back of the house so I can have a look around there?"

"Certainly," she said, and motioned for him to follow her.

Daniel remained a few steps behind her as they walked off the porch and around one end of the log house. Although he was absorbing the surroundings as they walked, he also couldn't help but notice the slight sway of Maggie Ketchum's hips. She was wearing a pair of faded Levi's that molded to her bottom like the seat of a worn saddle. A pale pink T-shirt outlined breasts that were rounded and full and jiggled ever so slightly as she walked. She was a voluptuous woman. The kind that men wanted in their arms and their bed.

He couldn't deny that he'd wanted her from the very first time he'd met her. But he'd carefully kept his attraction to himself. Daniel didn't get involved with women. Not in a serious way. After watching his mother go through the misery and degradation of being deserted by his father, Daniel didn't want any part of marriage or the responsibility that went with it.

But even if he hadn't been soured by Robert Redwing's behavior, even if he decided he had what it took to be a husband and father, he was smart enough to know that Maggie Ketchum was way out of his reach. She rubbed shoulders with the well-to-do. She could have most any man she wanted. There was no way she would ever want a Ute Indian, who'd grown up hard on the reservation and now lived modestly on a deputy's income.

"There's nothing back here, really," Maggie said, swinging her arm toward a wooden deck furnished with a group of redwood lawn furniture.

Pulling his thoughts back to the moment, Daniel glanced briefly at the back door of the house and the deck that was obviously used for family gatherings. He was more interested in the small gate that opened into a thick stand of ponderosa pine.

"Where does that trail go?" Daniel asked her.

Maggie glanced toward the quiet path that was cushioned by a thick layer of yellow pine needles.

"Oh, it goes for about a hundred yards, then dips down to a meadow where we pasture a few horses. A mare that I ride on occasion, her colt, then Aaron's gelding, Rusty, and then another gelding."

"Does Aaron ever go down to the meadow?"

"Sure. He goes there a lot. To visit the horses. And it's also his job in the evening to feed them their grain. This trail ends at a small barn. That's where we keep our saddles and tack. Aaron plays around there at times. But I went as far as the barn and called for him. He wasn't there."

Her voice trembled as she answered his questions. As Daniel watched her swallow and struggle to compose herself, it was like having a knife stuck in his chest, and the blade just kept twisting and turning.

The reaction to her pain was enough in itself to scare the hell out of him.

He didn't really know Maggie Ketchum all that well. He'd talked to her three, four, maybe five times on the telephone during the Rider investigation. Also, during those long weeks, he'd had two rather lengthy interviews with her. But even those visits had not given him much insight into the beautiful woman behind the sad blue eyes. Yet from the very first time he'd seen her, he'd felt an overwhelming attraction that had only grown over the past few months.

"What about the horses?" he asked. "Did you see all of them?"

"No. At the back of the meadow there's another grove of trees. When it's hot, the horses are usually back there for shade. But I didn't look, I took it for granted that they were there."

Daniel glanced down at her feet to see she was wearing a pair of sandals. "Maybe you'd better go change your shoes to something sturdier. I think we need to walk down to the meadow and take a look."

"All right. But what...what are you thinking? Do you think he's left on one of the horses?"

"If I were still a little boy and I wanted to run away, that's how I'd do it." Taking her by the shoulder, he turned her toward the house. "Get ready. I'm going to go use the radio to call in more help. I'll meet you back here in a couple of minutes."

Nodding, she ran toward the house. Daniel hurried

back to his vehicle to radio the sheriff's department back in Aztec.

A few minutes later he found Maggie waiting for him by the gate. She was wearing a pair of cowboy boots and had a crumpled straw hat on her head. He was glad to see she was composed enough to think of shielding herself from the elements.

"Three more officers are coming. They're going to comb the outer perimeters of the ranch, just in case he decided to go to a neighbor's place," Daniel told her.

Unlatching the wooden gate, he ushered her through. As they walked single file down the winding trail with Maggie in the lead, she said, "I just can't believe Aaron could be so spiteful. He's never given me any sort of problem. Not about obeying me...not with school...not anything."

"Maybe this time he was more hurt than you realized," Daniel suggested.

She didn't reply. But Daniel could see her hand swiping the region of her eyes. The sight touched him, and as they hurried down the trail, he prayed the boy would show up soon.

When they reached the barn, they could see the horses grazing some two hundred yards away in a far corner of the meadow. It took Maggie only a moment to scan the herd and announce that Aaron's horse, Rusty, was not among them.

"Let's see if his saddle is missing, too," Daniel suggested.

Maggie raced into the barn and jerked opened a wooden door to a small room where several saddles hung from ropes attached to the rafters. Bridles, bits, spurs, reins and other riding paraphernalia hung in neat rows along the walls. A stack of folded blankets and saddle pads filled one end of a crudely made counter running along the back wall of the small room.

"His saddle is gone," Maggie grimly announced. She went over to the stack of blankets and ran her hands along the folds. "So are his favorite blankets. Dear God, he's taken off on horseback! By himself!"

The idea that he'd gone off alone without her permission stunned Maggie, and all she could do was stare in disbelief at Deputy Redwing.

"Well, better that than going down to the county road and trying to hitch a ride with a stranger," Daniel told her.

He walked out of the barn and looked down at the hard-packed earth. There were very few discernable tracks, but as he moved out away from the structure, the soil became looser and he eventually spotted small boot tracks accompanied by a set of four matching horseshoes.

Careful to stay out of his way, Maggie followed a few steps behind him and tried to keep her tears at bay. She was more than frightened now, she was angry that her son could have done something so defiant and hurtful.

"It looks like he mounted up here and rode off toward the north," Daniel declared after a few moments. "Is there anything in that direction he might be going to? Like a cabin?"

Maggie shook her head. "No. There're only more mountains in that direction. Ross Ketchum, my brother-in-law, runs a few cattle up there in the dead of summer when the grass is on, but other than that there's nothing."

Daniel glanced up at the sun. "Aaron probably left when he told you he was going to see Skinny. That means he's been gone for hours. On a horse, he could have gotten far."

Maggie closed her eyes for a brief, painful second. "I know," she said hoarsely. "What are we going to do?"

"I think the best thing we can do is to saddle up a couple of your horses and try to follow his tracks. Are you up to it?"

The question prompted her to look at him. She'd only met Daniel Redwing a few months ago and she still wasn't sure whether she liked the man or not. He had a spare way of talking that often left her trying to read his mind, and when he looked at her with those dark-brown eyes of his, she felt very unsettled, almost feverish. But he was a good lawman. She'd heard Jess, her brother-in-law, praise him many times and right now her son's well-being depended on the man.

"Of course!" she answered. "But do you think we can catch up to him before dark?"

"Hopefully. If not, we'll get dogs and lights. We'll find him one way or the other, Maggie. Trust me."

Yes, she had to trust him. Right now he was the best hope she had of finding her runaway son.

Daniel quickly whistled up the horses, and in a matter of minutes they had saddled two mounts and were headed north into the mountains. Maggie was careful to ride a few steps behind the deputy as he leaned over in the saddle and scoured the ground for any signs of Rusty's tracks.

Most of the time the imprints were faint, and a few times they disappeared altogether, but somehow Daniel seemed to anticipate the route her son had taken and would manage to pick up the signs again.

As they climbed higher into the rough mountains, Maggie grew even more frightened for her son's safety. Especially with the sun dipping lower and lower in the western sky.

They continued to push the horses up the steep grade, and Maggie voiced her fears to Daniel. "There're bears up here, Daniel. If Aaron runs onto a cub and the mother is around, he'll—" She couldn't finish. The image was too gruesome to speak aloud.

"Bears are usually frightened by horses. I wouldn't worry about them too much."

She knew his words were meant to comfort, but they did little to relieve her fears. Deputy Redwing didn't have a wife or children. He didn't know what it was like to lose a spouse. Aaron was all she had. Now that Hugh was gone, he was the only thing she lived for. If something happened to him, she didn't think she would want to go on, or even could go on.

Up ahead of her, Daniel suddenly pulled his horse to a stop and held up his hand in a gesture for her to stop.

Maggie pulled on the mare's reins. "What's wrong? Have the tracks disappeared?"

"No. Something happened here. I need to get down and take a look."

Fear rose like bile in Maggie's throat, but she tried her best to swallow it down. "What do you mean something happened?"

Daniel climbed out of the saddle and Maggie quickly did the same. Keeping a tight hold on the mare's reins, she stood, waiting for him to explain. Instead he ignored her question as he stepped away from her and the horses and began to examine a nearby spot on the ground.

As she watched him squat on one knee and brush at the fallen leaves, she gritted her teeth and tried to be patient. But after a few more moments of silence, she said, "I hate to sound critical, but this isn't the Wild West anymore. Indian scouts and trackers have been replaced with technology."

Rising to his feet, he gave her a brief glance before he walked to another spot and carefully studied the ground. "Is that so?"

Her throat was unbearably dry, and she swallowed uselessly as she swiped a hand against her sweaty brow. "You know that it's so."

He came back to stand a few steps from her. Maggie breathed deeply through her nostrils as she studied his striking bronze features: the high cheekbones, the hawkish nose, the wide forehead and the strong squared jaws. He had to be somewhere near thirty, but when she looked into his eyes she saw a much older man, a man with all sorts of thoughts and secrets and dreams.

"Maggie, this land—these mountains have not changed in a hundred, even two hundred years. The horse your son is riding is still the same as the ones that outlaws and cowboys rode when New Mexico was still just a territory. Tell me, please, how technology is going to help out here, right now?"

Pink color tinged her cheeks. "Well, there are all sorts of things…like a helicopter."

Daniel shook his head. "I've already thought of a chopper. The forest is too thick, they'd never get a look through the canopy of trees."

"He might come out in the open," she suggested hopefully.

"He might. But I doubt it. Your son is on foot now. His horse has bolted."

She stared at him, not wanting to believe him, but very afraid he was right.

"Look, Daniel, I know that some Native Americans believe in visions. My sister-in-law, Bella, has a godmother who often 'sees' things, but that doesn't necessarily mean that you're capable of it."

The curve of his hard lips pressed into a thin line, and Maggie knew that she had offended him, but she couldn't help it. Now was not the time to use Indian folklore. Her son's life was at stake!

"I am a Ute. I'm personally not gifted enough to see things beyond my sight. But I can track most anything. There are signs on the ground here that tell me many things. They can't be ignored."

His firm, clipped words struck her like stones, and tears pooled in her eyes. She was ashamed that she had offended this man, and she was also very, very frightened. The combination was more than enough to make her break into sobs.

Drawing in a deep, shaky breath, she wiped her eyes with the back of her arm and fought off the urge to simply collapse. "I…I'm sorry, Daniel. Please…tell me. Tell me what you believe is going on with my son."

His brown hand wrapped around her upper arm, and without a word he led her over to the two areas he'd inspected a few moments earlier. "See, your son was standing here. There're the imprints of his boot heels. His horse was here beside him. You can see the tracks of the gelding's shoes where he stood. But then, here the ground is scraped where the hooves dug deep. The horse was spooked or agitated and took off at a gallop up the mountain."

Yes. Now that he'd shown her, she could see the story, too. "You're right," she replied as her mind whirled with possibilities, none of which was pleasant. "But couldn't Aaron have mounted up before the horse ran away? How do you know he's on foot?"

"Because the boot heels follow the horses tracks. See there?"

He pointed to a dim trail winding through the trees. The horse's hoof prints were visible to her, but not her son's. Yet she didn't argue with the deputy. She'd already learned her lesson about that.

"No. But I'll take your word for it." She turned her gaze on his face and suddenly she was acutely aware of his fingers pressed around her arm. He was standing only inches away and she could feel heat radiating from his body and the callused skin of his hand against her flesh. His dark face gleamed with sweat, which had also soaked a V shape on the chest of his khaki shirt. His arms and shoulders and thighs were all heavily muscled, and she instinctively knew that he was a strong man. Both physically and mentally. The fact helped to reassure her confidence in his ability as a lawman.

Concern darkened Daniel's brown eyes as they flicked over her face, and then slowly he reached a hand up to her cheek and pushed back a loose strand of red hair.

"You look very tired, Maggie. Why don't you stay here and let me ride on?"

She somehow managed to find the strength to straighten her shoulders. "No. You might need me."

He didn't say anything, but his fingers continued to rest against her cheek. His eyes probed deeply into hers.

Maggie couldn't speak. She felt herself being drawn to him. And though she tried to stop the forward motion of her body, she stepped into his arms, anyway.

He seemed to understand that she needed human contact and that she was longing for a pair of strong arms to hold her. He drew her deeper into the circle of his arms and, with one hand against the back of her hair, pressed her head against his shoulder.

"Oh, Daniel," she said with a broken sob, "I'm so scared."

"Don't. Don't cry, Maggie," he murmured. "Everything is going to be fine. Aaron is a strong boy, and he's comfortable with the outdoors."

The fabric beneath her cheek smelled of sun and wind and a faint musky scent that was utterly masculine and uniquely his. She drew it into her nostrils as her hands clung to his strong back.

"But...he's...he's still going up the mountain!" she exclaimed brokenly.

His hand slid up and down her back in a slow, soothing movement. "He has to be getting tired. He'll stop soon. And then we'll catch up with him."

She didn't make any sort of reply. She couldn't. Her throat was too choked with a jumble of emotions that weren't all to do with her missing son. Dear God, she prayed frantically, what was happening to her? Her son was somewhere in these mountains, alone and probably lost. How could she let her mind slip, even for a few seconds, to this man?

Guilt rushed through her like a shocking downpour of cold rain. "We, uh, we'd better be going," she stammered as she quickly lifted her head and backed away from him.

To her dismay, he caught her by the hand and prevented her from moving completely away from him.

"Not until I know that you're all right," he said.

A frantic wail bubbled up in her throat to nearly choke her, and she stared at him as though he'd just lost his senses. "All right? All right! Are you crazy? How could I be? My son is missing! These mountains go for miles and miles! There's nothing up here but wilderness—maybe a few mountain goats, elk and, God forbid, bear! Tell me, Daniel, am I supposed to be okay with that?"

He caught her by the shoulder, and though he didn't shake her, his fingers pressed firmly enough into her flesh to catch her attention.

"You're staying here. I'm going on alone," he said flatly.

Her mouth popped open to form a shocked circle. "Why?"

His face was grim, unmoving. "You're becoming hysterical. You'll be no good to me or Aaron like this."

Releasing his hold on her, he gathered up the gelding's reins and stuck his boot in the stirrup, but Maggie managed to grab him by the arm before he could swing himself up in the saddle.

"What are you, inhuman?" she demanded.

Lowering his boot back to the ground, he looked down at her, his features rigid except for one lone muscle ticking in his jaw. "I'm a lawman," he said in a clipped tone. "It's my job to keep a cool head."

"What about a cool heart?" she taunted.

For the past hours while he'd been in this woman's presence, he'd been fighting with himself to be a gentleman. Maggie was a lady. And he'd been telling himself it would only complicate things if he allowed himself to touch her the way he'd often dreamed about touching her. But her taunt had changed all that. He was no longer a gentleman. He was just a man.

Maggie continued to stand her ground, to wait for his answer, but it didn't come in the way of words. Suddenly his hands were on her shoulders, her breasts were crushed against his chest and her lips were captured beneath his.

Chapter Two

"Wh-what was…that for?" Maggie stammered breathlessly once he finally released her.

As Daniel looked at her, he realized he'd never seen a more erotic woman. Nor had he ever wanted one the way he wanted Maggie Ketchum. Her breasts were heaving and her lips were red and moist from his kiss. If circumstances were different, he'd kiss her all over again. And again. If she'd let him.

"To tell you I'm not just a lawman, Maggie. I'm a man, too. I can lose my cool. If that's what you want."

She'd never had a man speak to her in such a spare, blunt fashion. But then she'd never had a man kiss her like Daniel Redwing had kissed her, either.

"No," she quickly answered, then, glancing awkwardly away from him, she added in a subdued tone, "No. I want to find my son."

"Then mount up. And stay behind me," he ordered sharply.

Like a squaw walking behind her brave, thought Maggie furiously.

Trembling from head to toe, she gathered up the mare's reins and somehow managed to climb into the saddle. As she nudged the mare up the side of the mountain, she still couldn't believe the deputy had actually kissed her. Nor could she believe how she'd responded to him. Her body was still on fire and she knew her cheeks had to be crimson.

Instinctively her gaze was drawn to his back and the broad shoulders hidden beneath the taut khaki fabric. Did the man go around kissing every woman who needed the aid of a lawman? Forget that question, she scolded herself. The real question was, why had she ever fallen into the man's arms in the first place? Sure, she was upset. But there'd been plenty of times since Hugh's death that she'd been upset. And during those times she'd never so much as touched a man, much less kissed one.

Forget it, Maggie. You're under extreme stress. Besides, nothing matters now except finding Aaron.

As the horses climbed, the ground grew rougher. Several times her mare slipped, but managed to gather herself before she went to her knees. Thankfully Maggie was an experienced rider. Otherwise she might have fallen into the gorge far below to their left.

"The timberline is just ahead." Daniel tossed the announcement over his shoulder. "We'll stop there and let the horses blow. Once we get in the open, we might be able to catch a glimpse of Aaron or, at least, his horse."

Nodding, she followed Daniel to a spot on the mountain where the fir trees ended and huge, magnificent boulders protruded from the bald, grassy slopes.

Pulling the mare to a stop next to Daniel's mount, Maggie scoured the mountainside for any sign of her son. "I don't see anything. Not even any goats."

"His horse has been here. And not long ago."

Her heart leaping with hope, her gaze darted to Daniel's face to see his attention was focused on horse tracks surrounding one of the nearby boulders.

"What about Aaron?" she rushed the question at him. "Do you see his tracks?"

Frowning faintly, he said, "I'm not sure. Let's get down for a few minutes. The horses need to rest. They've had a hard, fast climb."

Maggie didn't protest. Even though she knew the waning daylight was precious, she was exhausted. Once she slid from the saddle and stood on the ground, her legs would barely hold her upright. Along with her misbehaving legs, her head was whirling at a nauseating speed.

Gripping the stirrup, she prayed for the rushing sound in her ears to stop and for the power to stand upright.

"Maggie?" Daniel asked softly. "Are you ill?"

She was drawing in slow, deep breaths in an effort to clear her head when his hand came against her back. His touch jolted her like an electrical current and the fire zapped her with a spurt of strength.

"No," she murmured. Then glancing up at him, she added, "I…I'm just really, really tired, that's all."

As he studied her weary face, his dark features remained stoic. Maggie wondered if he wanted to say, I told you to stay behind. But he didn't say anything of the sort. Instead he slid his arm around the back of her waist and clamped a steadying hand around her upper arm.

"Come over here and sit down," he instructed.

He helped her over to one of the boulders, and after she was sitting comfortably, he went over to his horse and slipped a canteen of water from the saddle horn.

Back at her side, he took off the lid and silently handed the insulated container to her. After she'd taken several long sips, he took the canteen and poured some of the cool water onto his handkerchief.

With one hand he reached up and pushed the straw hat from her head. With the other, he used the moist handkerchief to wipe her heated face.

"You're hot and dehydrated," he said grimly. "Why didn't you tell me you were feeling weak?"

His hands were big, yet extremely gentle as they touched her cheeks and chin, her neck and then her forehead. Maggie tried not to breathe in the scent of him. Tried not to think about the way his lips had felt against hers or the way he had tasted. Yet she couldn't stop her senses from registering everything about him.

"Because I knew we couldn't stop," she said in a hoarse whisper. We shouldn't be stopping now."

Her copper-colored hair was shoulder length and naturally curly. He pushed the wayward strands away from her cheeks and off her forehead as though she were his lover and the sweat on her face had come from their passion.

The notion caused her to shiver inwardly, and she closed her eyes and waited for him to pull back and put a few inches of space between them.

"Do you want Aaron to be raised an orphan?" he asked crossly.

Her eyes drifted open to see he'd taken a seat next to her and, though he was close, his gaze was not on her. His squinted eyes were scanning the bald, jagged crags of the mountain peaks.

"I'm not that weak," she protested.

Turning his gaze back to her, he silently studied her face until she felt the urge to squirm.

"What? What are you thinking?" she dared to ask him.

The corners of his mouth tilted up ever so slightly, and Maggie realized it was the first time he'd shown any sort of humor in her presence.

"That you are not exactly the woman I thought you were."

Maggie wasn't sure she should ask, but she did anyway. "What does that mean?"

One of his shoulders moved with a faint shrug. "The Ketchums are a tough crew. But you're not a Ketchum by blood."

She stared at him for a moment as she digested his words. "Oh. You thought—you think I'm just a rich, pampered woman."

"Not exactly pampered. But maybe a little soft."

His admission disappointed her, and that was frightening. Not since Hugh had Maggie cared whether a man regarded her highly. And it shouldn't matter how Deputy Daniel Redwing viewed her, either.

She swallowed as a knot of unsettled feelings gathered in her throat. "And what are you thinking now?"

"That you have grit."

Her eyes met his and she felt her heart thump with unexpected gladness. "Thank you, Daniel."

"You're welcome."

They were still staring at each other when Aaron's voice echoed through the mountaintops.

"Mom! Mom!"

Both Maggie and Daniel jumped to their feet and scanned the edge of the timberline where Aaron's voice seemed to have originated.

"That was him, Daniel! That was Aaron!" she exclaimed with excited joy.

"Yes. Here he comes now," Daniel said with a quiet smile. "To your right. See?"

A tiny whimper of relief passed her lips as she spotted her young son walking slowly out of the woods. He was leading Rusty, and from the looks of the flopping latigo he was fortunate to still have the saddle on the horse's back.

"Oh, thank God! Thank God!" she whispered hoarsely.

She started to run in her son's direction, but the ground was too rough and her legs too spongy to carry her safely. She stumbled several times before she finally managed to reach him, then, going down on her knees, she gathered the boy up in her arms.

For long moments she held her son in a crushing embrace as tears of relief streamed down her face. In turn, Aaron clung tightly to his mother until the excitement of being found eventually caused him to stir and talk in rapid, broken phases.

"Mom, I didn't mean to come this far! Something happened to the girth—I fell off Rusty. And he ran away. I've been chasing him...for a long time. I didn't think he'd ever stop!"

Taking him firmly by the shoulders, Maggie held her son out in front of her. He'd managed to hang on to his straw cowboy hat, but sweat and dirt streaked his freckled face and there was a long rip down the sleeve of his shirt exposing an equally long scratch on his arm.

"You weren't supposed to be on Rusty," she admonished. "You told me you were going down to the ranch yard to see Skinny!"

Aaron ducked his head with guilt just as Daniel walked up to mother and son.

"I know," Aaron mumbled. "But I...I wanted to go

camping. You know I did! So I filled up my saddlebags with food and tied on a bedroll. I was gonna come back tomorrow, Mom!" he reasoned, as though that made everything all right.

Maggie groaned and rolled her eyes up to Daniel who was desperately wanting to smile but was carefully hiding it in front of the boy.

"Oh, yeah," Maggie pointed out wryly. "After the bears ate you and spit out your bones. Aaron—"

"Gosh," the child interrupted as he suddenly noticed the man standing near his mother's shoulder. The shiny badge pinned to Daniel's chest and the pistol strapped to his hips were enough to make Aaron's eyes pop wide. "Am I in trouble?"

Daniel felt inclined to answer the child's question before Maggie had the chance. "Well, it appears as though you're in trouble with your mother. But not with the law," Daniel assured him.

The boy pushed the hat back off his head, then, using the back of his hand, he wiped his brow with an exaggerated gesture. "Whew!" he exclaimed with great relief. "I thought I was gonna be arrested for running off!"

Now that Maggie could see for herself that her son was well and truly safe, anger began to simmer where fear had once gripped her. "You'd better be glad your uncle Jess and Sheriff Perez are out of town," Maggie told him. "Or you would be in big trouble. Deputy Redwing has been tracking you for hours! He has other deputies looking for you, too. You've caused all sorts of trouble for a lot of people."

If possible, Aaron's blue eyes grew even wider as his gaze traveled from his mother's stern face up to Daniel. "Gee, I didn't know the law would come looking for me."

"Your mother has been very worried. Maybe you should apologize to her," Daniel suggested.

Aaron looked guiltily back at his mother and, with his chin sinking to his chest, he mumbled, "I'm sorry, Mom."

Releasing a heavy sigh, Maggie patted his back. Now was not the time for angry lectures. She was too relieved and overjoyed to have her son back safe and sound. Besides that, daylight was fading fast. They were going to have to hurry to make it back down the mountain before darkness settled in.

"All right, son," she said gently. "We'll talk about it later. But right now you should thank Deputy Redwing. If it weren't for him, you'd still be wandering around up here. Lost. You were lost, weren't you?"

Aaron nodded remorsefully. "Yeah. I didn't know where the heck I was," he admitted, then to Daniel he said, "Thank you, Deputy Redwing. I'm sorry I caused you so much trouble."

Even though Daniel was twenty-nine years old, he hadn't forgotten what it was like to be a little boy full of hurt and angry defiance and then later having all that pain turn into fear.

He patted the boy's slender shoulder. "I'm just glad you're all right, Aaron."

"You're not mad at me?"

Squatting, Daniel took hold of the boy's hand. "No. But I think you need to understand that a man's word is a very special thing. A good man doesn't break his word. So when you tell your mother where you're going, you need to make sure that you keep your word and do exactly what you told her. Understand?"

"Yes, sir. I will. I promise."

"Good." Daniel squeezed the boy's hand, then rising back to his full height, he glanced at Maggie to see a watery sheen in her eyes. "We'd better be going," he told her. "Dark is going to catch us."

Nodding, she said, "I'll go get mounted up. Can Aaron ride behind you? It looks like his cinch has just about had it."

"I'll be glad to have Aaron ride behind me," Daniel said.

The ride back down the mountain wasn't nearly as hurried as the trek upward had been. Aaron sat on the skirt of Daniel's saddle and kept his small arms wrapped tightly around the deputy's waist. At first the child was quiet and seemingly content just to be out of immediate trouble. But after a while the adventure of the moment caught up with him and he began to chatter with his rescuer.

Behind the two of them, Maggie carefully guided her mare down the rough trail and listened to the mostly one-sided conversation. Aaron had never been a bashful child, but she had to admit that she was surprised by her son's openness with Daniel Redwing. As far as she knew, Aaron had only met the man those two times he'd come to the house to interview her during the probe into Noah Rider's murder. Apparently there was something about the deputy that had gained her son's trust. Or maybe the fact that Daniel was a deputy explained Aaron's friendliness, she thought suddenly. Aaron was simply dazzled to be carried down the mountain by an honest-to-goodness lawman.

Just as she'd been dazzled to be kissed by one? Don't even think about it, she quickly scolded herself. That had been just a momentary lapse of her senses because she'd been so upset over Aaron. She didn't go around impulsively kissing men she hardly knew! Since Hugh's death, she hadn't kissed any man. Period. She hadn't wanted to.

On the way down the mountain, Daniel was able to pick up one of the deputies on his walkie-talkie and inform him that Aaron had been found and to spread the word among the other deputies and the ranch hands who were out searching.

Darkness had settled in by the time the three of them rode up to the little barn. While Daniel and Maggie worked to unsaddle the horses, Aaron's eyes darted from one long shadow to the next.

"Gosh, I guess I am glad I wasn't up there on the mountain in the dark. I thought I wanted to camp out by myself. But there might be mountain lions up there. Do you think they're up there, Daniel?" Aaron asked him as Daniel carried one of the three saddles into the tack room.

"Probably. I've heard several men talk about sighting them. And my grandfather used to hunt the big cats up in the southern mountains of Colorado. That's not that far away from us."

Standing close to Daniel's hip, Aaron looked up at him with childlike fascination. "Is your grandfather an Indian, too?"

"Yes, he's Ute. He lives on the Ute Mountain Reservation in Colorado. His name is Joe SilverBear."

"Does he hunt with a bow and arrow like the Indians used to a long time ago?"

Daniel's lips curved with amusement. "Sometimes. But he's getting older now. He doesn't hunt as much as he used to."

Aaron turned toward his mother. "Wow! Did you hear that, Mom? Daniel says there's big cats on the T Bar K!"

"Yes, I heard." Maggie stepped into the tack room carrying a handful of bridles. "That's one reason you'd better not ever try this camping thing again, young man," she added sternly.

Daniel fastened the saddle to the swinging loop of rope, then reached for the breast collar Aaron was holding. As he hung the piece of leather and mohair roping on a nearby peg, he said, "Aaron, if you really want to go camping that badly, maybe your mother will let me take you some time. Do you like to fish?"

At first, Aaron was so surprised by the deputy's suggestion he could only stare at him with wide, wonder-filled eyes. Then he looked at his mother and the words began to burst excitedly past his lips. "Mom! Did you hear that? Daniel said he'd take me camping! And fishing!" His eyes sparkled as he looked back at Daniel. "I love to fish and I'm good at it, too! Once I caught two trout at one time!"

Daniel actually chuckled. "Sounds like you've already learned how to tell fishing stories."

"That's not a story! That's the truth," Aaron insisted, then turned pleading eyes on his mother. "Mom, can I go? Can I?"

Maggie thoughtfully began to hang the bridles in their usual places along the wall. She didn't know what to make of this new development. A few minutes ago she'd been feeling a little guilty because she'd refused to allow Aaron to go on the camping trip with the boys' club in town. She hadn't realized just how upset she'd made him. But that didn't mean she wanted her son to go on such a personal outing with Daniel Redwing. She hardly knew the man. And she didn't even want to try to imagine what his motive in this might be. Still, she was reluctant to upset Aaron all over again. And she certainly didn't want to offend Daniel after he'd gone to such lengths to find her son.

"I'm sure Deputy Redwing has very little time away from his job. It might be a while before he could take you camping," she gently warned.

"That doesn't matter. Just, can I go?"

"We'll see," she said, using the vague promise to pacify him for the moment. "Right now I want you to run ahead and get in the shower. I'll be along shortly to fix supper."

Aaron looked anxiously over at Daniel. "Are you leaving soon?"

Daniel reached out and patted the boy's shoulder. "I'll stop by the house to say goodbye."

The child's eyes suddenly lit with anticipation. "Okay!"

He leaped through the doorway of the building and took off at a dead run up the trail to the house. Turning toward Daniel, Maggie shook her head in a hopeless gesture.

"I'm so sorry about all this, Daniel. I've caused you and the department so much trouble. Thank God you didn't have helicopters out looking."

"I'm just glad we found him safe and sound. You were very lucky. I guess you know that."

Nodding, she suddenly felt as if the darkness was swallowing them up, cocooning them in the little barn. With Aaron gone they were totally alone, a fact that Maggie couldn't push from her mind.

"Yes," she murmured. "All the way down the mountain I kept thinking of the hundreds of things that could have happened to Aaron. And I kept thinking, too, that maybe—well, if something had happened to him, it would have been my fault. I guess I should have allowed him to go on the camping trip.

It certainly wouldn't have been as harmful as what might have happened today."

Frowning, Daniel stepped over to where she stood. "Look, Maggie, you were right earlier. I don't have any children. I can't tell you or anyone how they should raise their kid. But I believe you can't allow a child to have his own way all the time just to keep him from running away. That isn't any sort of discipline."

Her gaze dropped to the toes of her boots. "No. You're right. But I feel so guilty." She lifted her eyes back to his. "I'm sure you've already guessed that Aaron doesn't have a whole lot of male companionship. Oh, there's Skinny and the other ranch hands and there are his uncles, Ross and Jess, and their cousin Linc, but he doesn't get to spend any serious, intimate time with any of them. They're all so busy, and I guess none of them ever stop to think that Aaron misses having a father."

"Does Aaron remember his father?"

Shaking her head, Maggie turned and began to straighten the bridles she'd hung on the wall. "No. Aaron was too small to remember anything when Hugh was killed. Sometimes I think that's the worst part about it. I have my memories to hold on to, but Aaron doesn't have anything. He doesn't even know what it's like to have a father."

Daniel placed his palm upon her shoulder because he wanted to comfort her and because standing so close to her made it impossible for him not to lay a hand on her in some way.

"Neither do I," he admitted quietly. "But I made it. So will Aaron."

Quickly she turned to face him. Her eyes were wide with surprise, her lips parted. "You...you didn't have a father?"

Oh, yes, he'd had a father, Daniel thought bitterly. At least for a brief time. Not that there'd been anything fatherly about Robert Redwing. The only thing he'd had to do with Daniel was to sire him. While Daniel was still a young boy the man had left his son and his wife, Pelipa, and headed south to Arizona. He'd become a drunk and a thief and served several stints in the state penitentiary before he'd eventually died in a car wreck while trying to evade the police. Yes, he'd had a father for a few brief years of his life. But he didn't want to tell Maggie Ketchum about a man who'd brought pain and shame to his family.

Instead of responding to her question, Daniel nudged her toward the door. "It's late. I've got to get back to the department and do some paperwork before I go home."

He obviously didn't want to answer, and Maggie respected his privacy by not pushing him. Even so, she realized she wanted to know more about this man. And that in itself was a scary idea. For seven long years her heart, her body, had been dormant. Men had tried to spark her interest, but she'd felt nothing toward any of them. Mostly because she hadn't wanted to feel anything. Not with Hugh still living in her heart. And now this man, this dark, handsome Ute had come along and stirred up all kinds of emotions in her.

"Of course. Let's get to the house," she said, wondering why she suddenly felt the urge to cry.

Quickly, before she could make a fool of herself, she started out the door only to have his hand wrap around her arm and tug her back inside the small, dimly lit building. Maggie looked up at him, her brows arched, her heart pounding.

"Maggie, before we go…I wanted to—" He let out a heavy breath, dropped his hand from her arm, then caught hold of her again. "I don't know how to say this. I just wanted you to know…earlier today—in the mountains when I kissed you—I wasn't trying to insult you."

Her breath came soft and fast as she tried to search his face in the waning light. "I never thought you were."

His fingers tightened ever so slightly on her arm. "I don't go around kissing women like that. You, uh, well, you got me off track there for a moment or two."

She tried to smile, to ease the crackling tension between them. "I'm flattered that an older woman like me could distract you, Deputy Redwing."

His fingers eased to slide slowly up her arm and onto her shoulder. Once they reached her hair, he twined the curly strands around his fingers. Maggie shivered inwardly at the intimate contact.

"You look very young to me."

"I'm nearly thirty-four," she replied.

"And I'm twenty-nine."

Up until this moment Maggie had stood motionless, but now she unconsciously edged closer to him. "So tell me why a healthy twenty-nine-year-old man doesn't go around kissing women?"

His lips formed a wry line. She made kissing sound like such a normal, simple thing for him to do. But he'd never viewed the act as simple. Getting that intimate with a woman was something he mostly tried to avoid. As much as he liked the feel of a soft female in his arms, he didn't want to give himself a chance to get that close, to need or want anyone the way his mother had wanted and pined for his father. Yet when he stood here so close to Maggie, everything but her seemed to leave his mind.

"Because I haven't found a woman I've wanted to kiss," he answered quietly. "Until now."

She drew in a sharp, sudden breath. "What kind of line is that?"

Suddenly both his hands were on her shoulders, and he was drawing her forward, circling her body with his strong arms. The air rushed out of her lungs as she planted her palms against his broad chest.

"It isn't a line, Maggie. I've wanted to do this from the very first time I saw you."

"Daniel—"

His hand lifted to her cheek where he rubbed a gentle, enticing circle. "Say my name again," he whispered. "It sounds so good coming from your lips."

She was trembling, shaking with a need that left her voice hoarse, her mind whirling. "Daniel, I…"

With a soft groan he bent his head, and anything else she might have said was swallowed up by the probing search of his lips.

This time their kiss was different. This time the fear for her child's safety wasn't racing through her mind. This time there was nothing standing between them. Not even a breathing space.

At some point during the embrace, he pulled her tightly against him, and Maggie groaned as her full breasts pressed against his chest, her hips aligned with his. Mindlessly her arms slipped around his waist, her mouth opened in hungry response.

For the next few moments Maggie allowed herself the rich pleasure of being in Daniel's arms, of having his hard, warm lips roam recklessly over hers, having his hands touch her with love.

Love? Love!

The one word racing through her mind was enough to make Maggie rip herself from his embrace and back away as though he were one of those mountain lions his grandfather hunted and she was the prey.

"Maggie…" he began in a perplexed voice.

He stepped forward only to have her hold up a hand to ward him off.

"Don't, Daniel," she pleaded hoarsely. "Please don't touch me again."

He stood still, his hands dropping to his sides. "Why?"

She groaned and then made a lunge for the door. "I'm sorry, Daniel. I'm just not ready for this," she mumbled in a choked voice.

"Maggie!"

Ignoring his call, she stepped out of the little barn and hurried up the trail to the house. Her legs were weak and wobbly, and several times she almost fell upon the dark, winding path. But she stumbled on, determined to put as much space between herself and Daniel as she could before he decided to follow.

Thankfully, the lights from the house eventually flickered through the pine trees, and, breathing a sigh of relief, she slowed her pace. When she entered the back door, she could hear Aaron's shower click off. Knowing the child would soon be dressed and heading to the kitchen to eat, Maggie hurried to her own private bathroom and began to splash cold water on her heated face.

After a few moments her cheeks began to cool and her senses calm somewhat. As she washed her hands, she stared in stunned horror at her disheveled image in the mirror.

Maggie had never been a vain person. It didn't matter to her if her hair got mussed or her face smudged. There were far more important things in life than trying to look perfect. So she was hardly shaken by the fact that her hair was tangled, her shirt dirty and snagged with a three-corner tear on the shoulder. It was the dark desire shadowing her eyes, her swollen lips and the excited color on her cheeks that totally stunned her.

Dear God, she looked like a woman who'd been making love to a man!

Chapter Three

"Mom! Where are you?"

"I'm coming." Tossing down the towel, Maggie drew in a deep breath and hurried out to the kitchen.

When she entered the room, Aaron was pouring himself a glass of milk, and thankfully, as he chugged it down, he seemed not to notice that there was anything amiss about his mother.

"It's so late that supper will have to be soup and a sandwich," she told him as she began to pull plates and bowls from the cabinet.

"Okay. Can I have bologna and mustard?"

"You may."

By the time she'd gathered the dishes together,

she'd managed to focus her attention on the task of preparing a light supper. But before she started, she walked over to where her son was standing by the cabinet counter and put her forefinger beneath his chin.

Tilting his face upward for inspection, she examined his spiky, wet hair, his neck and ears and finally the bramble scratch on his arm.

Aaron began to squirm impatiently. "I'm clean, Mom. And I'm okay."

"You have a bruise on your cheek and a scratch on your arm. We'll deal with the scratch after you eat," she promised, then with a weary sigh she patted his wet head. "We're lucky that's the only thing that happened to you."

Satisfied that her son was clean and all in one piece, she opened the pantry and took two cans of vegetable soup from a shelf. As she emptied the contents into the saucepan, Aaron plopped down in a chair at the breakfast table and thoughtfully watched his mother's jerky movements.

"Are you really, really mad at me?" he asked in a cowed voice.

She glanced at her son as she stirred water into the soup. Since Aaron had never done anything nearly as serious as running away, she really didn't have a clue as to how she would punish him. And right now, dealing with his misbehavior was only a part of her problems.

"I'm not sure what I am, Aaron. I was very scared when I couldn't find you."

His expression was remorseful, but not nearly enough to suit Maggie.

"Well, Mom, you should have known I wouldn't get hurt," he said with just enough cockiness to warrant a glare from his mother.

"How did I know that, young man?"

"Well, you know that I can ride Rusty better than anybody on the ranch. Even Skinny," he boasted.

"Is that why you fell off?" Maggie asked as she placed the pan of soup onto the gas burner.

Clearly insulted, Aaron exclaimed, "Aw, Mom! I—"

Before he could finish, a knock sounded on the kitchen door. Maggie opened her mouth to tell Aaron to answer it, but she was wasting her time. Aaron shot out of the chair like a bullet and raced to the door.

"Mom! It's Daniel!" he shouted as though she were deaf.

"Don't just stand there looking at him. Let him in," she instructed her son.

Aaron flung the door wide. "You can come in, Daniel."

"Thank you, Aaron." With his hat in his hand, he stepped into the kitchen and glanced toward the other side of the room, where Maggie was stirring something on the gas range.

"Mom's fixing soup," Aaron explained. "You can stay and eat, too. If you'd like. We have plenty of bologna."

"Aaron! Please!" Maggie scolded softly.

Aaron shot his mother a perplexed look. "Well, he can, can't he? I thought we're always supposed to share with company."

Turning away from the stove, she glanced at her son before turning a strained smile on Daniel. "Sorry," she apologized. "He doesn't understand that bologna isn't something you offer a guest."

As Daniel looked at her, one corner of his mouth lifted into a faint grin, and Maggie felt her heart skip into a rapid dance against her rib cage. It wasn't right that the man looked so good to her—too good, in fact.

"I don't know why not," Daniel told her. "I think it's pretty tasty stuff."

Maggie released a breath of air she hadn't realized she was holding. "Then why don't you wash your hands here at the sink and I'll have everything on the table in just a few minutes."

He moved farther into the room with Aaron glued to his side.

"I wasn't hinting to be fed supper," he said, unable to pull his eyes away from her.

Jolted by the fact that he was so near to her again, she turned back to the soup. "I know you weren't. But you're welcome to join us. Offering you a sandwich is the least I can do after all you've done for me and Aaron."

Staring at her for a few more moments, Daniel wondered why she didn't want to look at him, why she had run from him after kissing him so deeply, so sweetly. It didn't make sense to him. But then, Daniel didn't know much about the way a woman's mind worked.

Even though he'd often dreamed of how it might be to have a family, a real family that stayed together and loved each other through thick and thin, he'd never actually pictured himself in the role of husband or father. A man had to know about a thing before he could be good at it, and Daniel had been taught very little about love. Especially from a father who'd lacked any sort of morals, decency or human kindness.

"Come on, Daniel." Aaron grabbed his forearm and urged him toward an open doorway to their right. "I'll show you where the mudroom is. It's easier to wash your hands in there."

The two males entered the small utility area and as Daniel washed his hands at a deep galvanized sink, Aaron sidled up to him and said, "I'm worried about Mom. She's acting strange. Like she's sick or something. Do you think me running off has made her sick?"

Daniel glanced through the open doorway of the mudroom. From this position, he could see Maggie standing at the gas range. Her shoulders were slumped, her head slightly bent. She had to be exhausted, he thought. He was certainly feeling the long ride and he was accustomed to straddling a horse. Yet he figured her quietness had nothing to do with her fatigue. She was upset with him because he'd kissed her. And probably even with herself because she'd kissed him back.

Glancing down at the boy's troubled face, he said gently, "No. I don't believe your mother is ill. I think she's very tired. You put her through the wringer, you know. You should be a little ashamed of yourself."

Grimacing, Aaron hung his head. "Yeah. I guess I am," he mumbled contritely, then suddenly his head jerked up and he shot Daniel a bright smile. "But I'll make it up to her. I'll do all sorts of chores and she won't even have to ask me! Just watch!"

Aaron dashed out of the mudroom and over to his mother. By the time Daniel joined them, the boy was busy placing plates and utensils on the table.

"Is there something I can do?" Daniel offered as he stood beside her at the range.

Maggie darted a glance up at him, then quickly turned her attention back to the boiling soup. His nearness made her tremble as though there were an earthquake inside her, and she deeply resented the fact that he had such a powerful effect on her. It wasn't supposed to be that way. She wasn't supposed to be feeling anything for this man.

"No. I think everything is ready. Go ahead and take a seat."

He put his hand on her shoulder. "Are you all right?" he asked in a low voice.

Without looking at him, she said stiffly, "Yes. Yes, I'm fine."

Daniel glanced around to see that Aaron was still at the table and out of earshot. "Maggie, about that kiss—"

"I'm not going to talk about that!" she interrupted in a rushed hush. "Not here! Not now!"

Frowning thoughtfully, Daniel studied her bent head. "When?"

Her head jerked up, and she stared at him in dazed wonder. "Never! That's over—and it won't happen again!"

She reached up and switched off the burner beneath the pan of soup. Daniel dropped his hand, but he didn't move away.

"Never say never, Maggie Ketchum."

Something like fear filled her blue eyes. "It's time to eat," she said hoarsely.

Picking up the soup, she carried the pot over to the table and began to fill the three bowls that Aaron had set out. The boy was obviously thrilled to have Daniel share the simple meal with them and he made a big issue of showing Daniel where to sit and fetching him a cold soda from the refrigerator.

Once they were eating, Aaron dominated the conversation and Maggie was relieved. She didn't want Daniel to have a chance to turn his attention to her. It was hard enough on her nerves just having him sit across the table from her, much less having him talk to her. Especially when he'd already said more to her than he should have. And done more than he should have, she thought wretchedly.

Halfway through the meal, the telephone rang and Maggie went to answer the portable instrument sitting on the end of the cabinet. The caller was her sister-in-law, Victoria. While she assured Aaron's aunt that her nephew was safe and sound except for a scratch and a bruise, she covertly watched her son and Daniel at the kitchen table. The two of them were talking with easy familiarity as though they were old buddies or even relatives. The notion was unsettling. It wouldn't do for her son to get close to this man. Not when she planned on making a swift and permanent break with him after tonight.

"That was your aunt Victoria," Maggie said to Aaron, once she returned to the table. "She was getting ready to come over here to check you out, but I told her you only had a scratch and a bruise."

Aaron swallowed down a mouthful of potato chips before he said to Daniel, "Aunt Victoria is a doctor. She's just had a baby. He's a boy, but he's too little to play with. He still drinks from a bottle and he wets his pants. Ugh!"

Daniel smiled fondly. "Yes, I've met little Samuel."

Aaron looked at him with surprise, then dawning. "Oh, I forgot. You work with Uncle Jess."

"That's right."

"See, Mom, Daniel has a badge just like Uncle Jess's." The boy reached over and nearly touched the shiny, oval emblem pinned to Daniel's khaki uniform. "It says San Juan County, New Mexico, on it. That's where we live. And Daniel is the law all over this land."

"Daniel isn't the law, he *enforces* the law," Maggie corrected him.

Aaron scowled at his mother. "I know that. He can put handcuffs on people and take them to jail."

And that ability was obviously impressive to a nine-year-old boy, Maggie realized.

"He has a Colt .45, too," Aaron went on with enthusiasm. "That's the kind of pistol he likes to carry—just like in the Old West—like Blackjack Ketchum toted. And he was our kin!"

Maggie stared at her son, unwilling to believe the stuff that was rolling out of his mouth. "Aaron! You have no idea what sort of gun Blackjack Ketchum used! And he certainly wasn't our relative! Where did you hear such a thing?" she demanded.

"Well, Skinny told me about the gun. And the kids at school tell me all the time that Blackjack was my kinfolk. And he might be, Mom. You don't know," he argued.

Daniel chuckled, and Maggie lifted a helpless gaze toward the ceiling.

"Eat your sandwich," she ordered Aaron, then seeing Daniel had finished the food on his plate, Maggie asked, "Would you care for coffee and a piece of pound cake?"

Daniel figured she was more than ready for him to leave, but he was going to deliberately ignore her wishes. After tonight he probably wouldn't get the opportunity to share this sort of time with her or Aaron. He had to make the most of these moments.

"Sounds good."

"What about me?" Aaron chimed in. "Can't I have cake, too?"

"Cake, but no coffee," Maggie told him as she

rose from the table. "And then you're going straight to bed."

Aaron's freckled nose wrinkled up with disappointment. "Aw, heck, I want to talk to Daniel some more."

"I'm sure Daniel is all talked out by you."

Daniel glanced over to where Maggie stood at the cabinet, but she had her gaze focused on the long loaf of cake she was slicing.

"Aaron hasn't talked me out. But I do have to be leaving soon," he announced.

"How come?" Aaron asked with frank innocence. "Don't you want to stay and talk to Mom a little more?"

"Aaron!" Maggie sternly warned.

Daniel could hardly keep from flashing a grin at his new little buddy. "I can't think of anything I'd like to do better. But I have work to finish tonight. Maybe I'll get to talk to her another time," he said just as she was placing the plate of cake in front of him.

Pausing at his shoulder, Maggie looked down at him. The warm suggestive signals in his brown eyes seemed to arc straight into her, flooding her limbs with heat and her cheeks with color.

Nervously she wiped her sweaty palms down the front of her thighs. "Uh…do you want cream with your coffee?"

"No. Black is fine."

She served Aaron his dessert, then went back to her seat and tried to pour all of her attention into the piece of cake in front of her. But she could hardly choke down more than two bites. She wanted—no, she needed for the meal to be over and for Deputy Daniel Redwing to be gone. Otherwise, she would be unable to keep her eyes from straying to his lips and her senses from remembering every reckless second she'd spent in his arms.

Glancing down the table, she noticed Aaron's eyelids were beginning to droop and the movement of his fork was growing slower and slower. The long, traumatic day was catching up to him, and now he was about to fall asleep right in his plate.

"Aaron, I really think you're too sleepy to finish your cake. Why don't you say good-night to Daniel and go to bed," she gently suggested.

His mother's voice stirred Aaron from his sleepy stupor and he lay down his fork and climbed out of his chair.

"I guess I'd better," he reluctantly agreed, then to the surprise of both adults, he went over to Daniel and circled his arms around his neck. "Good night, Daniel. And thanks for not taking me to jail. I promise not to ever run away again."

Daniel had never had any siblings. Nor had he been around children very much in his life. He hadn't known it was possible to become attached to one so quickly or to be touched so deeply by such unconditional affection.

Patting the boy's back, he said, "That's good. I'm going to hold you to that promise. Good night, Aaron."

Yawning, the child ended the hug and left the kitchen. Once he was out of sight, something inside Maggie snapped and tears began to stream down her face.

Seeing her swipe at them, Daniel got up from his chair and went around the table to where she sat.

Touching the crown of her hair with his hand, he said quietly, "Maggie. What's wrong?"

"I'm sorry," she said, her voice rough with tears. "All of a sudden it struck me. Today I could have lost him. And I couldn't have lived through that. Not after Hugh. Aaron is a part of him, and he's all I have now."

"But you didn't lose him," he said, then, easing onto the edge of the chair next to her, he clasped both her hands in his. "I understand today has been hard on you, Maggie. But it's over. And in the long run, I believe this little episode has taught Aaron a lesson."

Breathing deeply, she struggled to curb her tears. "I'm not so sure. He's unhappy with me."

One corner of Daniel's lips lifted to a wry smile. "Aaron adores you."

"Yes. But he wants a father, too. And I…I just can't give him that. Not now. Not ever," she whispered fiercely.

Daniel didn't know what to say. He could hardly admonish her for not wanting to marry again. Not when he'd sworn to avoid the role of husband for as long as he walked this earth. To take on a spouse was like holding a person's happiness in your hands. The responsibility was just too great. He didn't want to fall short in some woman's eyes and then see them fill with tears of misery.

Daniel had watched his father make mistake after mistake with his mother. And too many times during his childhood he'd watched tears of sadness roll down Pelipa Redwing's face. Daniel could still remember the helpless feeling he'd had as he'd tried to comfort his mother, to love her enough to make up for all of Robert Redwing's shortcomings. He'd not been able to make his mother happy, and it would be foolish of him to think he could make a wife happy.

After a moment he said, "I think you're exaggerating the problem with Aaron. He seems like a happy, balanced child to me."

She leveled a sardonic look on him. "Yeah, so happy that he ran away."

Wishing in some way that he could absorb her pain, he squeezed her soft hands. "He wasn't trying to run away from you. He just wanted to spend the night in the woods. If you ask me, that's a pretty natural urge for a little boy."

Dropping her gaze from his face to their entwined hands, she murmured, "You should never have offered to take him camping. He'll be pestering you about it from now on."

The tangled curls dancing around her head were a myriad of red shades, Daniel decided, as his eyes slid over the silken mass. Sparks of copper, gold, chestnut and mahogany were spun together to make one brilliant color. It was beautiful, vibrant hair, like a flame beckoning him to touch its warmth.

He pushed his mind to their conversation. "I wasn't just telling Aaron that to appease him. I really will take him camping."

"No!"

The one, softly spoken word was out before she could take it back and he stared at her with slightly raised brows.

"Why?"

Her lips twisted and then she glanced away from him. "Because I…I don't think it would be a good idea."

"Why? Because I'm an Indian—a Ute?"

Maggie's head jerked, her gaze collided with his. "No! How could you ask such a thing? You being Ute has nothing to do with it!"

Both his shoulders lifted and fell in a negligible gesture. "I never know with some people. And there has to be some reason you don't want your son around me."

Awkward heat filled her cheeks and warmed them to the deep pink of a wild rose. "Oh, I think you know, Daniel."

He studied her for long moments and after a while she swallowed as though something was choking her. Daniel could have told her she wasn't the only one with a tight throat. His was knotted with feelings he'd never encountered before, and deep inside him, where no one could see, he was shaking with fear.

Dear God, he was a lawman. He faced dangerous people with guns and knives and every sort of weapon they could get their hands on. But none of them had shaken him the way this woman did.

"Because you think I might use your son to get to you?" he asked bluntly.

Slowly, deliberately, she pulled her hands from his and rose from the chair. Daniel watched her walk over to the sink and stare out the small window above it.

"I don't think that...exactly," she eventually answered.

With a rough sigh, Daniel rose from the chair and walked over to stand just behind her. He desperately wanted to put his hands on her arms or shoulders—anywhere, so long as he was touching her.

"What are you thinking?" he quietly prodded.

The nearness of his voice surprised her. She whirled around and braced her hands behind her on the edge of the sink. "I—right now it's obvious Aaron has a bit of hero worship for you. You're not only a rough, tough lawman to him, you're also the hero who saved him from bears and mountain lions and—"

Daniel held up his hand to interrupt her tumble of words. "I haven't done anything heroic. The only thing I've done today is my job."

Well, almost everything had been his job, Daniel thought wryly. Those kisses he'd shared with Maggie hadn't exactly been a deputy's duty.

A worrisome grimace wrinkled her forehead. "Aaron doesn't see it that way. And if he—spends more time with you—especially doing something special like camping—he'll—well, he'll get attached to you."

Daniel's features were as smooth and unmoving as stone as he closely studied her. "And that would be bad?"

Her eyes darted away from him to settle on a spot on the tiled floor. "I didn't say anything about it being bad. It would just be—problematic."

He told himself it would be foolish to take her words in a personal way, but he could hardly keep from it. To think that she didn't want him around her child was insulting, even hurtful. Especially after she'd been more than willing for him to search for her son.

"For whom?" Daniel asked softly. "You?"

Irritation puckered her brow as she looked up at him. "No! This is all about Aaron."

"Is it?"

She heaved out a frustrated breath. "Yes, it is. He's just a little boy with a great big heart. He would get to liking you, and then he would start to…to love you."

The last was added in a whisper as though she could hardly bear to repeat the word to him. Which was just as well because Daniel could hardly bear to hear it.

Love. Except for the affection he'd received from his mother, he'd never been loved. Not really. It was silly of this woman to think her son could ever *love* him.

"I think," he said after a few silent seconds had

passed between them, "that you're making giant leaps for no reason. We were talking about one night of camping and a day of fishing. Not an emotional attachment for life. But even if we were, why should that bother you? Don't you want Aaron to get close to people?"

Surprise flickered in her eyes and then she began to stammer, "Daniel…that's not…what I meant. And I—" She turned her back to him and continued in a strained voice. "Please. I'm very tired. I just don't want to talk about it anymore."

She was dismissing him and though he wanted to stay, he knew it was time for him to go, to get back to his own world, far away from this rich widow with the sad blue eyes and sweet, sweet lips.

Tired himself now, he turned and retrieved his hat from where he'd placed it on the floor by his chair. After he'd tugged it down over his forehead, he walked to the door and paused to look at her. Her back was still toward him, the rigid line of her stance sending him a cool, distant message that cut him in a way he didn't understand.

"All right. I'm going, Maggie. But before I do, I think you should hear something. Maybe you don't want or need a man in your life, but your boy does. He needs someone he can admire and respect and build a bond with."

Guilt and pain twisted in her chest like a piece of barbed wire, until finally she whirled around to face him. "Like who?" she flung at him. "You?"

His features stiff, he opened the door. "No. Not me."

She watched him step through the opening and into the warm night. It wasn't until the door clicked quietly behind him that something hit her. Something deep and awful and lonely.

Chapter Four

A little more than a week later Maggie was sitting in a room at the Aztec General Hospital, reading the *Farmington Daily Times* to an elderly man who was recovering from a stroke.

"Looks like our area is still in a drought alert, Mr. Alvarez. Here it says we're at least twelve inches below normal for the year. Let's hope there are not any lightning fires anytime soon or we'll all be in trouble."

The man nodded that he understood and agreed with what Maggie was saying. She read a bit more about the worrisome drought, then turned to the sports and the baseball standings. She was about to tell Mr. Alvarez that the Colorado Rockies had won last night when her name suddenly came over the hospital intercom.

"Maggie Ketchum, report to the nurses' station, please."

As she placed the newspaper to one side, Mr. Alvarez shook his head. The old man never wanted her to leave the room and she couldn't blame him. The visits he'd had from his family were few and far between.

She touched his hand and smiled gently. "Don't worry. I'll be right back. We haven't gotten to the comic strips yet."

Maggie hurried out of the room and turned left to head down a wide corridor toward the nurses' station. As her feet skimmed over the polished tile, she glanced at her wristwatch. It wasn't quite eleven. Maybe the hospital was running low on help today and they needed her to help serve lunch.

"Hannah, did I hear my name called?" she asked the nurse sitting in a desk chair behind the long L-shaped counter.

The middle-aged woman dressed in colorful scrubs glanced up. "You sure did. You have a telephone call on line three."

She placed the phone on the counter, punched the button and handed the receiver to Maggie.

Turning her back for a measure of privacy, Maggie spoke, "Hello, this is Maggie Ketchum."

"Hello, Maggie. This is Daniel."

He didn't have to add the Redwing. She would have recognized his voice anywhere, anytime. And the mere sound of it caused her breath to catch in her throat.

Unwittingly her hand fluttered up to her throat as she said, "Daniel. How are you?"

"I'm doing fine. What about you?"

She closed her eyes as the past few days paraded through her mind. Aaron hadn't given her a minute's trouble, but she'd spent most of the time worrying about her son. And thinking about the deputy on the other end of the line.

"Everything has been going okay." Wariness crept into her voice, even though she was trying to sound as casual and nonchalant as possible. Her mind was spinning, wondering why the man had called her, and at the hospital, of all places.

"I'm sorry if I'm interrupting your work," he said, breaking the silent tension between them. "But Jess told me I might catch you at the hospital."

"Yes. I volunteer three days a week. It gets me off the ranch, and I like helping people."

"I have no doubt that you enjoy helping people, Maggie."

His last words were spoken in a gentle tone, as though to imply he knew her intimately. The idea warmed her cheeks and she glanced around to see two young nurses casting her furtive glances.

Clearing her throat, she turned away from their sly glances and said, "Uh, was there something I could do for you, Daniel?"

"Well, actually, I need to talk to you."

Her stomach fluttered. "I...what are—"

"It's about Aaron," he said, interrupting her stumbling words.

"Aaron has been fine," she quickly replied. "I haven't had any trouble with him. In fact, he's been bending over backward to do things he knows will please me. I've allowed him to walk back down to the ranch to visit Skinny, and so far he's returned to the house promptly. I'm thinking that runaway he pulled was his first and his last."

There was a long pause on the line during which she could hear Jess yelling something in the background to one of his deputies and she wondered with a bit of chagrin if her brother-in-law had put Daniel up to making this call. Since Jess and Victoria had married and Ross and Bella had tied the knot, the whole family seemed to think she needed to find a beau.

But that thought quickly flew from her head. Daniel didn't seem the sort of man to be manipulated. Even by his boss.

Finally he spoke, "I hope you're right, Maggie. That's why I feel like we need to talk. Can you meet me for lunch at the Wagon Wheel at about twelve-thirty? If nothing else comes up, I should be free by then."

Meet him for lunch? That was the last thing Maggie should do. The man definitely had too much effect on her. But how could she politely decline when he wanted to discuss her child's welfare? It would seem negligent if not insincere.

"All right. I'll see you there at twelve-thirty," she told him.

"Good," he said, hanging up.

Slightly dazed, Maggie turned slowly and hung the receiver back on its hook.

Hannah studied her pale face. "Trouble?"

Maggie mentally shook her head and tried to pull her scattered senses together. "No. No trouble at all. Just a little something I need to take care of." She wasn't about to confess to the other woman that the chief deputy of San Juan County wanted to meet her for lunch. The nurse would be on the hospital grapevine before Maggie could walk back to Mr. Alvarez's room.

The next hour and a half passed slowly for Maggie. She finished reading the *Times* to Mr. Alvarez and then walked down the hall to visit a young woman who'd gone through an emergency appendectomy the day before. By the time she left the hospital to walk the short distance downtown to the Wagon Wheel, her stomach was tied in knots and she kept trying to convince herself that she wasn't the least bit happy about seeing Daniel again. But as she walked her heart sang and the corners of her mouth tilted into a subtle smile.

When Maggie entered the diner, she spotted him waiting on a bar stool. He noticed her immediately and she stood to one side of the entrance and waited for him to walk over and greet her.

"I'm glad you could make it," he said, his eyes

sliding warmly over her face. "Do you want to sit at the bar or in a booth?"

Maggie quickly scanned the busy room. Ranchers, businessmen and -women and longtime locals filled the tables, booths and bar stools lining the long Formica-covered bar.

"I'd like a booth, but it looks like we've stepped into the middle of the lunch rush. We might have to grab whatever we can find," she said.

He inclined his head toward the back of the room. "I see a waitress cleaning a booth," he said. "Let's go for that one."

He took her by the arm and led her toward the opposite end of the café. Maggie could feel glances being darted at them, but she wasn't surprised by the interest the two of them were creating. Daniel had a presence about him that would make anyone look twice, and she was a Ketchum, a family that was always targeted for gossip.

Today Daniel was dressed for work. His khaki shirt with its San Juan County Sheriff's Department emblem on the sleeve was tucked into a pair of dark blue Wranglers. The black high-heeled cowboy boots he was wearing made him seem that much taller than his six-foot frame, and the pistol strapped to his hips reminded Maggie that he was a man who sometimes put his life in the line of fire.

At the booth Daniel helped her into the vinyl bench seat, then took his place directly across from her. As they waited for a waitress, he allowed his gaze to travel leisurely over her face and the parts of her that weren't hidden by the table. She was wearing a coral-colored blouse over a pair of white slacks. The pale smooth skin of her chest and throat peeked out from the open V of her blouse. Her curly hair tumbled like a red waterfall onto her shoulders and he felt himself reacting to her beauty in a totally primal way.

For the past week and a half he'd told himself that he needed to avoid this woman. She could cause him some major heartache if he allowed it to happen. Yet here he was, sitting across from her and enjoying every second of having her near.

"I'm sure you're wondering what this is about," he said finally.

Her delicate brows pulled together as she glanced at him. "Actually, I am. I haven't had any trouble with Aaron. And—"

He held up a hand to stop her tumble of words. "I haven't had any trouble with Aaron either. But I'm worried about him. I thought you should know."

Maggie's blue eyes widened just a fraction. "Worried? I don't understand. Just because he ran off the other day, doesn't mean he'll do it again. I've had a long discussion with him about it and I truly think he's sorry for his behavior."

Daniel's expression remained stoic. "Aaron's jaunt into the mountains isn't what I'm here to talk to you about."

Surprise parted her lips. "Oh?" she questioned warily.

A rueful look suddenly crossed his dark features. "Aaron has been calling me," he said bluntly. "Every day, at least once or twice. Sometimes at home. Sometimes at work."

Maggie's jaw dropped with shock at the same time her heart fell like a heavy rock to the bottom of her feet. Aaron had been calling this man? It didn't seem possible. Even though Daniel had rescued him from the mountains, her son didn't know the deputy well enough to be calling him, period, much less daily, she thought.

She couldn't stop the groan in her throat. "Oh, Daniel, I'm so sorry. I had no idea this was going on. But you can bet his telephone privileges will be taken away immediately. You won't be bothered with this again."

He opened his mouth to make a reply when a waitress suddenly appeared beside their table. Impatient as she was to hear what he had to say, Maggie didn't prod him to speak. This conversation was about her son and she wanted it kept private.

"What can I get for you two?" the young woman asked as she cast furtive glances back and forth between Daniel and Maggie. "You want to look at a menu or get the blue-plate special today?"

"What is it?" Daniel asked.

The lanky blonde looked at him as though she'd like to sit on his lap and recite the whole menu, which was an extensive one for a diner. But in spite of her obvious eyelash batting, Daniel didn't seem to notice her effort to flirt. Which surprised Maggie. Most every man alive liked to flirt, even those that shied away from marriage.

"Beef tips and noodles. English peas and scalloped potatoes."

"That will do for me. Put an iced tea with it," he said. "What about you, Maggie?"

"The blue-plate will be fine with me. And I'd like coffee, please."

The waitress pulled out a pad and pencil and scribbled down their order. Once she'd moved on to another table, Maggie scooted up on the edge of the seat and leaned toward Daniel.

"Like I said before, Daniel. I'm really sorry about this. I'll talk to Aaron immediately."

His bronze features remained unmoved as his brown eyes searched her face. "No. That's not why I'm here…to have you scold him."

Maggie's brows lifted to faint question marks as her mind whirled with questions. "But he needs to be disciplined."

A slight frown wrinkled his forehead. "Why? Because he called a friend? He wasn't committing a sin, Maggie."

Perhaps not a sin, Maggie thought. But Aaron's behavior had caused her to meet with Daniel, had caused her to see his face and wonder what it would be like to kiss him again. As far as she was concerned that was close to a sin.

She drew in a deep breath and let it out slowly.

"Okay. Then if you're not here to complain about the phone calls, just what is it that you want to tell me?"

His eyes said he pitied her, and the look caused Maggie to stiffen her spine.

"That your son is lonely. He's craving something. And I think he believes I can give it to him."

"Lonely!" The word burst past Maggie's lips and for a moment she forgot they were in a public place with people seated all around them. "For God's sake, Aaron isn't lonely! He has people near him all the time."

He didn't say anything. Instead he looked at her quietly, solemnly, as though he was trying to understand her but couldn't. She'd never had a personal relationship with a Ute or any other Native American and she wondered if they all spoke in the same spare way that Daniel did.

"Sometimes a man can feel lonely even if his house is full of people."

Maggie understood exactly what he meant. When Hugh had died there had been people all around her, hugging, kissing and reassuring her that she would survive her grief. But she'd been detached from their presence. Her heart had been craving her husband's company. Was Daniel trying to tell her that Aaron's heart was craving something, too?

With a heavy sigh she glanced toward the front of the room just in time to see the waitress approaching with their meal. Slipping back against the cushioned seat, she tried to collect herself as the young woman placed the plates of food on their table.

Once the waitress was gone, she slipped a hand into her hair and pushed it back from her forehead. "Daniel, this is so—embarrassing. What has my son been saying to you? Has he told you that he's unhappy?"

Daniel frowned thoughtfully as Maggie picked up her napkin and spread it across her lap,

"Not in so many words," he said.

At least she could be relieved for that much, Maggie thought. "Then why do you think he's calling you?"

He picked up his fork and stabbed it into a chunk of roast beef. Maggie watched him for long moments until she finally told herself that she had to eat, also. She couldn't just sit here and stare at him.

But, damn the man, he was just so big and strong, even more so than she remembered, and seeing him again was filling her with all sorts of feminine longings that she'd believed were long dead.

"He wants to talk about the camping trip and—things in general," Daniel said. He wasn't about to lay everything out to this woman at one time. Just hearing that Aaron had been making the phone calls had obviously shocked her. What would she think if he told her that the boy was longing for a father and he resented the fact that Maggie wasn't looking for one?

"But you haven't scheduled a camping date," she argued. "What is he doing, begging you to take him?"

A wry smile slanted his lips. "Maggie, sometimes the planning is just as much fun as the doing. It's fun for Aaron to talk about the things we might do together."

Together. Maggie latched on to that one word and tossed it around in her head like a cat with a mouse. She realized that Aaron had wanted to go camping ever since Daniel had brought up the subject. He talked about it incessantly and he'd even asked her if she would call Daniel and make a date to go. Maggie had continually put her son off, telling him that they couldn't pester Daniel when he had such important work to do.

Apparently Aaron had gone behind her back and taken the task of calling Daniel into his own hands. She didn't know whether to be worried about her son or very, very angry, or both. Obviously, he wanted to be with Daniel, and she didn't know what to make of that.

Nervously she licked her lips and reached for her coffee. After a careful sip, she said, "This has floored me."

"You shouldn't be worried, Maggie. As far as I can see, your son is just being a normal boy."

Even though she was far from hungry, Maggie pushed her fork into the pile of peas on her plate. "Oh, yeah, making a pest of himself. Calling a man he hardly knows at his workplace! I guess you're thinking I'm not much of a mother," she said dourly.

"I don't know. Are you usually home when Aaron comes home from school?"

Her fork stopped in midair as she stared at him with resentment. "Of course I am. Do you think I neglect my son?"

He didn't look up as he continued to eat. "Not neglect. More like misunderstand."

She gasped at his bold arrogance. "I guess now you're going to tell me that *you* understand him better than his own mother?"

"Sometimes it takes an outsider to see things."

Maggie's blood began to simmer and the feeling amazed her. Other than the scare Aaron had given her the other day, she couldn't remember the last time she'd felt so angry and stirred up about anything.

"You're talking like you have visions that tell you things about my son. But you told me that you don't have those. Visions, I mean. So how can you *see* all this stuff that I supposedly can't?"

He shook his head ever so slightly and looked at her with exaggerated patience. "I don't have visions, Maggie. Not every person with Native American blood running through his veins is a magical medicine man or a prophet. I'm just using common sense."

"I thought you'd never had children," she blurted sharply.

The squint of his eyes told her she'd stepped into a place he wouldn't allow her to go.

"I haven't had a child," he said coolly. "But I was a boy once. I know what it's like to yearn to explore the outdoors. Thankfully my mother didn't cosset me."

Unlike you. He might as well have said the words. She could feel them hanging in the air between them like menacing storm clouds. Her first reaction had been to bark back at him, to put him in his place and maybe, just maybe see some sort of emotion cross his face.

"Maybe your father wasn't killed like Aaron's," she said with a hint of bitterness.

His nostrils flared but that was the only emotion she could see on his face as he continued to eat.

After a long pause, he said, "He was killed. A few years after he deserted my mother and me."

She suddenly felt awful, and every word that came to her mind sounded too trite to say out loud. "Go ahead," she said ruefully. "Call me the B word. I deserve it."

A tiny frown pulled his brows together as he glanced up at her. "You're only thinking of your son. I understand."

She wished he didn't. And she wished she could take back all the sharp words that she'd spoken since they had taken their seats.

With a heavy sigh she said, "I'm sorry, Daniel. I realize that at times I'm…unreasonable. Especially where Aaron is concerned. I don't know—" She glanced away from him and shook her head. "Hugh's death changed me. For a long time I was afraid to let Aaron even step out of the house." She turned her eyes back on his face to see he was watching her intently, as though he wanted to know everything she was feeling and thinking. The idea struck emotions deep inside her and she found it difficult to go on. In a slightly hoarse voice she said, "I guess I was desperately afraid that I would lose the only thing I had left of Hugh."

His eyes probed hers. "You loved him very much," he stated.

Dropping her head, Maggie nodded. "Very much."

"That's good. That's the way it is supposed to be," he said.

Something about his simple words released the tightness in her chest, and she looked up at him and smiled. "Yes. You're right. And I'm learning to let go. It probably doesn't seem like it to you, but I am. Little by little."

He went back to eating, and Maggie tried to do the same. After a while he said, "Aaron is a good boy. I care about him. That's why I called you. I want to keep the promise I made to him and take him camping."

Maggie didn't want to give in. She didn't want her son to get involved with this man. Not when she could feel the sexual tension between them sizzling like a fuse on a stick of dynamite. But she had to stop and remind herself that Aaron had been talking with Daniel daily. He was *already* involved with the man. Trying to keep them apart now would only make matters worse.

"If you're sure that's what you want to do. Then it's all right with me."

He glanced across the table at her, and Maggie could see a faint flicker of surprise in his brown eyes.

"Something is wrong. I expected you to argue about this."

Maggie nervously licked her lips. "Well, I'm not. It's obvious that this is important to Aaron. And maybe once he gets past this camping thing, he'll settle down."

Daniel wasn't so certain about that. Aaron's problem couldn't be solved with just one camping trip. But he wasn't about to go into it now with Maggie. Getting her to agree to this much was enough for now. Besides, he really couldn't give her the sort of advice she needed to deal with Aaron's needs. The boy wanted male companionship. He wanted a father. And God knew that Daniel didn't know one thing about having a father or being one.

"Okay. I'll try to have everything ready to go by this coming weekend. We'll drive over to Navajo Lake. Ever been there?"

Maggie nodded. "A long time ago. It's beautiful."

"I'm glad you think so. Maybe you'll enjoy the trip, too."

Her heart stopped as she looked at him with wide eyes. "Me? I won't be going!"

He looked at her in his quiet, inspecting way. "I need for you to go."

"You're a big, strong man, Daniel. And Aaron isn't a baby. He knows how to brush his teeth and wash his hands and all that sort of thing. You don't need a woman tagging along and getting in the way."

"I don't expect you to get in the way. I expect you to join in. Having you along will be good for Aaron. And I want to make sure you're along so that I don't allow him to do something you might frown on. This way I can relax and you won't have to worry, either."

Relax! That was a laugh. Spending the weekend with Daniel Redwing would be the furthermost thing from relaxing. She could already see him now, standing at the lake's edge, naked to the waist of his blue jeans as he cast a line. She'd be staring at him like she'd never seen an unclothed man before. And all the while she'd be thinking, wanting to relive the kiss he'd given her.

Putting her fork down next to her plate, she said, "Look, Daniel, I'm not really an outdoor person. I'd be a nuisance. And I'm not worried that you'll allow Aaron to do anything foolish. You're a lawman after all, you ought to know the rules of safety."

Ignoring her reasoning, he said, "I assure you, Maggie, you'll have your own tent and all the privacy you need."

Did he think she was opposed to going on this trip because she was worried he might make a sexual overture toward her? How embarrassing! It wasn't him she was worried about but herself.

"That part doesn't concern me. I just think it would be better if…I didn't go."

He shook his head, and Maggie's heart sank. She'd already learned he was hardheaded and stubborn. More than likely if she didn't agree to this trip, he'd call it off. And once Aaron learned of that, he'd be one hurt boy.

"The only way I'll go is if you come with us. Take it or leave it."

Daniel didn't know why he was being so insistent about Maggie going with him and Aaron. She was not a woman he could allow himself to get close to. She was far out of his league. And even if she'd been one of his own kind, he couldn't permit himself to think of her as anything but a friend. For years now, ever since he'd been old enough to realize how his father, Robert Redwing, had destroyed his mother's life, Daniel had vowed to never take a wife or have children. He didn't want the chance to hurt or disappoint a family in the way his own father had.

But the boy had touched him, and the attraction he felt for Maggie was something he couldn't stop. Even with keeping his hands to himself, it would be a pleasure just to look at her and have her company.

"You drive a hard bargain, Daniel Redwing."

His mouth slanted to a faint grin. "My grandfather taught me to be persistent."

She laughed softly. "And my father taught me to be flexible. He always said it takes a man that will bend to get things done."

Daniel's heart leaped with a strange and sudden joy. "Does that mean you agree to come along?"

"I suppose," she said, and though she wanted to be reluctant about it, she couldn't ignore the excitement rushing through her. She sipped her coffee and studied him over the rim of her cup. "You'll have to tell me what I need to bring for this trip."

Daniel avoided looking at her. Just in case she

might pick up the joy in his eyes. "You won't need to bring anything. Just yourself."

"And Aaron," she added, as though she needed to remind them both for the reason of the trip.

Clearing his throat, he kept his gaze on his plate. "Yeah. And Aaron," he replied.

Suddenly her fingers were touching his free hand that was lying atop the table, and the jolt from the connection jerked Daniel's head straight up.

"Thank you, Daniel, for going to all this trouble. Most single men have—well, they have other things to do over the weekend."

If she was thinking that he normally entertained women over the weekend, she couldn't have been more wrong. But Daniel didn't bother to correct her. Maybe it would be safer to let her think he was a bit of a playboy and not a man she should sidle up to.

"It's no trouble, Maggie." He pulled his hand away from hers and pointed to her plate. "You'd better eat up. I've got to be back at the department in fifteen minutes."

Chapter Five

The next day Maggie drove to her sister-in-law's health clinic in Aztec, where she volunteered two afternoons a week. Usually she organized patient files, typed reports and opened mail.

Today she'd just finished typing a letter of referral for a man needing knee surgery when Nevada Ortiz walked into the small office where she was working and placed two foam cups of coffee on the desk.

"Break time," she said cheerfully.

Maggie glanced at her wristwatch. She'd been typing for two solid hours. "Oh. I didn't realize so much time had passed."

"You've had your head down all afternoon. I seriously doubt I'd dedicate my time and energy to my sister-in-law the way that you do."

Nevada Ortiz was a young, pretty nurse who'd devoted the past few years working as Victoria Ketchum's nurse. Her hours were long and irregular and many of the patients were stressful to deal with, but Nevada had an inherent ability to calm even the most unruly person.

Gesturing toward the stack of mail she'd been working on, she said, "This is much better than slouching around the house, searching through television channels. I need to be busy and productive."

Nevada took a seat on a molded plastic chair sitting in front of Maggie's desk and picked up the black coffee. "Well, so do I. But that doesn't mean I want to work all the time. I've been thinking I might drive up to Durango for the weekend and do some shopping. Want to come along? We could even go wild and do one of those spas," she suggested with a wink.

Maggie couldn't remember the last time she'd gone out of town for the weekend to shop or anything. Except for her volunteer work, she was a homebody.

"Thanks for asking me, Nevada, but I've got other plans."

The young woman with a mass of black curls floating around her head and complexion the color of smooth café au lait looked at Maggie with interest. "Really? That's good to hear. Victoria's always grumbling that you won't do anything fun."

Was this weekend going to be fun? Maggie wondered. The word sounded ridiculous. She was nearly thirty-four years old. Fun was for the young and the single.

You are young and single, Maggie. You can't be a widow for the rest of your life.

The little voice in her head was unsettling, and she sipped her coffee as she did her best to shake it away.

"I don't know how much fun camping will be. But we'll see."

"Camping?" Nevada frowned. "I've never heard Victoria say anything about you being an outdoor woman. Other than horseback riding. What's brought this on?"

Maggie sighed. "Aaron, of course. Little boys need things like this, Nevada. Believe me, once you have a few children of your own you'll find yourself doing all sorts of things you never thought you'd do. I just hope to God you have a husband around to help you."

Nevada waved her hand in a dismissive gesture. "Not me, Maggie. I don't want to think about kids or marriage for a long time. I watched my mother grow old and worn-out taking care of an abusive, cheating husband. That's not for me."

Maggie grimaced at the young woman. "Marriage isn't always that way, Nevada."

Nevada looked a bit rueful as she glanced at Maggie. "Maybe not. But it's work. And I have enough trouble taking care of myself. Besides, I like playing the field. You don't get bored and cranky that way."

Rolling her eyes, Maggie sipped her coffee. "Nevada, one of these days you're going to meet someone who's really going to break your heart."

Tossing her head, Nevada smiled smugly. "I'm too smart to let that happen."

"Well, why wasn't I invited to this party?"

Both Maggie and Nevada looked around to see Victoria entering the small office. She was a tall, dark-haired beauty with a slim figure that belied the fact that she'd given birth to a son only a few months ago.

"We thought you were working," Nevada said. "Where's Mr. Langley? Are you finished with him?"

Victoria nodded. "All finished. I decided not to give him a shot today. His blood tests looked good and he's feeling better." She walked over to the small desk where both women were seated and eased her hip onto one corner. "So what are you two hens gossiping about? Your latest boyfriend, Nevada?"

The young nurse giggled, then looked across to Maggie. "I'm going to keep him a secret for a while. But Maggie is off for a wild weekend. She's going camping."

Surprise marked Victoria's expression as she twisted her head around to look at her sister-in-law. "Are you? Where? Who with?"

Maggie lifted her gaze to the ceiling. She hadn't planned on mentioning the outing to anyone, except for maybe Ross and Bella, who might miss her and Aaron if they were gone from the ranch for a whole weekend. "Lake Navajo. Deputy Redwing promised to take Aaron, and I…I'm tagging along, too."

"Maggie! That's wonderful news!" Victoria exclaimed.

Nevada straightened up at the edge of the plastic chair. "Deputy Redwing! You're spending the weekend with Deputy Redwing?" she asked incredulously.

Maggie nodded. "Why? What's wrong with him?"

Nevada let out a dreamy sigh. "Nothing. Absolutely nothing. He's such a hunk, and I've tried every way I know of to catch his attention, but—" she paused and shrugged her shoulders with defeat "—he just seems to look right through me."

"Well, there's no need to be concerned, Nevada. Daniel is just a friend who's helping me out with Aaron. That's all there is to this little trip." She didn't go on to tell the women about Aaron making a pest of himself by calling Daniel every day. Her child's behavior was a private thing and she'd tried to handle it that way. After her lunch with Daniel, she'd gone home and had a long, stern talk with her son. He'd promised her that he would never call Daniel unless he had permission first, and so far he'd kept his word. Maggie could only wonder if his promise had lasted because he'd finally gotten what he wanted—a camping trip with Daniel.

"Hmm. I don't know of many men who'd do such a thing," Victoria murmured slyly.

Maggie frowned at both women. "There're plenty of men who volunteer their time to help needy kids. Daniel's gesture isn't any different."

"Oh, come on, Maggie. Give us a break. You don't expect Victoria and me to believe Deputy Redwing has no personal interest in you," Nevada drawled mockingly.

"Even if he did have some sort of personal interest in me, I wouldn't let anything…happen between us." She turned a pleading eye on Victoria. "You understand me, Victoria, tell her that I've sworn off men."

Victoria nodded solemnly. "That's right, Nevada. Sadly, the whole family has tried to get Maggie interested in dating again. But it's more important to her to cling to my brother's ghost than to build a new life with someone else."

Stunned that Victoria could make such a callous remark, especially in front of a friend, Maggie gasped out loud. "Victoria! How could you say that?"

The beautiful doctor, who also happened to be her sister-in-law, shook her head glumly. "Because it's true. That's how."

Before Maggie could say anything to defend herself, the receptionist appeared in the doorway. "Dr. Hastings, can you take on one more patient today? She looks like she feels terrible."

Maggie didn't know why Victoria took the trouble to glance at her watch. She would care for the woman even if it kept her here until midnight.

"Of course, Gloria." She turned her gaze on Nevada. "Go put her in an examination room and check her vitals. I'll be there in a minute or two."

Even though her break had been less than five

minutes, Nevada didn't complain or question. She jumped to her feet and hurried off to take care of the sick woman.

Maggie set her coffee cup to one side and reached for another piece of mail. "Well, I'd better get back at it, too," she said as she ripped the envelope with a letter opener.

"Uh, Maggie, before I go, I—" she paused and smiled brightly at her sister-in-law "—I just wanted to say I'm glad that you're going on this outing with Deputy Redwing. He's a very nice man. Quiet but strong. When Jess was shot and close to dying, he helped me keep my head together, among other things."

Maggie's eyes fluttered to the desktop as an uncomfortable heat filled her cheeks. "Yes. Daniel is…very good in difficult situations."

"And he might be good for you."

Maggie's head jerked up. "Oh, no. Don't start that, Victoria. This is all for Aaron and Aaron only."

"Maybe it's time for you to start thinking about more than just your son."

Victoria turned and left the office before Maggie could come up with any sort of reply to that, and after a moment she released a long, heavy breath she hadn't even realized she'd been holding.

Victoria and Nevada could make what they wanted out of this camping trip, she thought crossly. She wasn't hunting for a man. And she was darn sure she'd never allow herself to love another one. She'd be crazy to set herself up for more of the pain she'd been through these past years.

Saturday morning dawned bright and beautiful without even a puff of a cloud to threaten the blue sky. By seven-thirty that morning Maggie had herself and Aaron ready to go and by eight she'd stacked their bags on the front porch for Daniel to load into his vehicle.

"Let's sit on the porch, Mom. That way we'll be ready to go when Daniel gets here," Aaron told her as she scurried around the kitchen making sure everything was as it should be before she closed the house.

"All right. You run on, and as soon as I get my purse I'll be out there," she told her son.

He raced away and Maggie left the spotless kitchen and walked down the hallway to her bedroom. She didn't know why she felt the need to look at herself one last time before Daniel arrived. It wasn't like she was going to a beauty contest.

Standing in front of a cheval mirror, Maggie eyed herself critically. As long as she couldn't see her backside, the tight-fitting jeans she'd decided to wear were flattering. The baby-blue T-shirt she'd topped them with was soft and loose and hid the curve of her small waist and full breasts. That, of course, was the main reason she was wearing the garment. The more she kept hidden from Daniel the better off they'd both be.

Leaning closer to her image, she checked the faint

gloss she'd applied to her lips. It was the only makeup she'd put on this morning and, though a little more color would have helped her image, she'd refused to doll herself up for a camping trip, or for Daniel.

Sighing, she turned away from the mirror, grabbed her purse and hurried out to join Aaron on the front porch.

Her son had been a bundle of excitement all morning, and even now he wasn't sitting quietly in a lawn chair. Instead he was swinging on the front gate and peering down the dirt road for any sign of dust stirred by Daniel's approaching vehicle.

"Mom, it's fifteen after eight. Daniel's not comin'."

Maggie didn't know whether to laugh or cry at her son's eagerness to be with Daniel Redwing. It was good to see him smiling and happy and excited. There'd been times the past few months she'd caught him when he was unaware, and the sad wistful expression she'd seen on his face always cut right to her heart. Aaron meant more than anything to her, and if camping with Daniel made him happy, she was willing to play along.

"He said he'd be here at eight-thirty, Aaron. Just be patient. Now get down from the gate. You're too big to be riding it. You'll have it sagging on its hinges."

"Aw, Mom, I can't ever have any fun," he complained. But he jumped from the gate and trotted over to where she sat in a wooden lawn chair.

Maggie playfully ruffled his hair. "Did you tell

Skinny that someone needs to be up here to feed the horses today and tomorrow?"

"Yep. He's gonna do it himself," Aaron said proudly. "He said he couldn't let just any old ranch hand take care of Rusty."

Thank God for Skinny, Maggie thought. He was the closest thing to a grandfather that Aaron had, and the old man had taught her son a lot about horses and cows and ranching in general. Skinny realized that someday Aaron and his cousins would have to take over the reins of the T Bar K, and when that time came, none of them could be greenhorns.

"Here he comes!" Daniel suddenly shouted as a plume of red dust appeared in the far distance. "That's him, Mom. You'd better get up and get your bags!"

"Aaron—" Maggie let the rest of her sentence drop as she watched her son race to the front gate as fast as his legs would carry him.

Daniel arrived in a dark-colored four-seater pickup truck. Before he could open the door and jump to the ground, Aaron was standing just outside waiting to greet him.

"Daniel, you're finally here!" he said with a happy grin.

Daniel leaned down and shook the boy's hand. "How's my little buddy?"

Aaron's face beamed with joy. "I'm really ready to go fishing. Mom got me some new lures. They're orange and green. And we got one for you, too. Just in case you'd like to try one."

Daniel smiled at the boy all the while he was acutely aware of Maggie ambling toward the yard gate. She was dressed casually in a T-shirt and jeans. Her thick, red hair was pulled back into a high ponytail, and gold hoops glinted at her ears.

She managed to look sweet and sexy at the same time, and when his gaze caught hers she smiled softly.

The tender greeting slammed him and turned his whole insides to mush. Just the weak sort of reaction he wanted to start the day with, he thought crossly.

"Good morning, Daniel."

"Good morning. Have you been waiting long?"

"Oh, we've been waiting a long time," Aaron said. "Mom had everything ready by seven-thirty."

It was all Maggie could do to keep from groaning out loud at her son's remark. "He's excited," Maggie tried to explain.

"That's good."

The two of them stared at each other for long seconds until Daniel finally began to tug on her elbow. She looked down at him and hoped the flushed heat on her cheeks was invisible.

"C'mon, Mom! Let's get our bags. We're wasting time."

"Okay, son." Maggie looked questioningly at Daniel. "Are you ready for this?"

"Don't worry, Maggie. It's my pleasure."

Pleasure. Pleasure! That's exactly what she felt when she was around Daniel Redwing, Maggie thought a few minutes later as they were driving off the ranch property and turning onto a main county road.

Even though there was a backseat, perfectly comfortable for either her or Aaron, Daniel had insisted there was plenty of room for the three of them up front. Then Aaron had begged to sit next to the window so he could look out. Maggie was now sandwiched between the two of them, struggling to keep her shoulder and thigh from pressing into Daniel's.

"Have you been to Navajo Lake?" Daniel asked Aaron.

Aaron wrinkled his nose thoughtfully and looked to his mother for answers. "Have I, Mom?"

"No. I don't think so. Your father and I drove past it once. But that was before you were born."

Maggie could still recall those few quiet minutes that she and Hugh had stopped and looked out over the glimmering lake. It had been one of the few times they were away from the ranch together. He'd driven her up to Colorado Springs to a cutting-horse show, and while they were there he'd purchased a horse just for her. She'd cherished the palomino gelding until Hugh had died, then the memories had made it too difficult to ride the horse. She'd eventually sold him and tucked the money away for Aaron's college fund.

"Well, you're in for a treat, then," Daniel told him. "The water is deep blue and there're slabs of rocks to climb and sit on. And pine trees for shade."

Aaron leaned up in the seat to look at him. "What about bears? Did you bring your gun?"

Daniel shook his head. "My firearm is only for work. We don't need a gun to go camping."

Aaron was suddenly wide-eyed at Daniel's reasoning. "But if a bear gets after us—he…he might kill us!"

An amused smile crossed Daniel's lips. "Don't worry. They're more scared of you. We'll put away all our food and not invite one into camp. Besides, I wouldn't kill a bear."

This statement floored Aaron even more. "Why not? They're mean!"

"The bear is a sacred animal to the Ute. To respect his spirit will make you a stronger man."

Aaron silently mulled over Daniel's statement for several long moments, then he said with childlike wisdom, "Oh. That's kind of neat. I guess you like bears the way I like horses."

Daniel chuckled softly and Maggie glanced over at his profile. "See what you're in for all weekend? You'll be wishing you had a nickel for all the questions you answer."

"I'll be fine," he said to Maggie, then turned his attention to Aaron. "I don't exactly like bears the same as horses, Aaron. For a Ute the bear is to be respected, and the horse is to be valued and admired."

"Well, I sure value Rusty," Aaron exclaimed. "I wouldn't sell him for a thousand dollars or two thousand or a whole stack of money!"

"I'm glad you love your horse that much," Daniel told him. "That's the way it should be."

Aaron began to chatter about some of the other horses on the T Bar K and how Skinny was teaching him to nail on a horseshoe and rasp their hooves. Maggie didn't pay close attention to her son's words, she was too busy dreaming, wondering what it would be like for her and Aaron to have a man in the house, for them to be a true family again. Daniel was so good with him. Gentle, yet firm.

"Mom! Mom! Daniel asked you a question!"

Aaron's shrill voice penetrated her thoughts, and she glanced guilty around at Daniel. There was a faintly amused look on his face and she wondered if the man could read her mind. Dear Lord she hoped not. Otherwise, she couldn't face him. "Uh, sorry, I was…thinking. What did you ask?"

"If you brought a swimsuit."

"Yes. Aaron begged me to bring our suits. But we both know the water will be too cold for swimming."

Daniel's brown eyes glinted. "We'll see."

Before long Daniel was steering the truck onto Highway 64 and then north on a smaller highway. For miles the road curved and climbed through high arid country dotted with sage and ragged juniper. Eventually it opened up to low, rock-strewn mountains and dark-green cedar trees.

When the lake finally appeared, Aaron was quick to shout. "There it is! Wow! Just look at all that water!"

Daniel took his eyes off the road just long enough

to point out the dam. "We're going to drive across it. You won't be scared, will you?"

Aaron puffed out his chest. "Shoot no! I'm not scared of anything."

Maggie rolled her eyes and shot Daniel an amused look. "What about bears and spending the night alone in the mountains?"

The child wrinkled his nose. "Well, other than those two things," he corrected.

"Is this where we'll be staying?" Maggie asked of Daniel as the truck started across the huge, earthen dam.

Over to the right she could see a huge marina and several other buildings. Vehicles and boat trailers filled the massive parking area while out on the lake, sailboats and small fishing craft bobbed upon the blue waters.

"I think we need to talk about that. Once we get across the dam, I'll pull over."

What was there to talk about? Maggie wondered. They needed to find a tent site and set up everything to make a camp.

To her surprise Aaron wasn't frightened by the height or narrowness of the road crossing the dam. He was completely awed, even after Daniel pulled over onto a wide graveled area built for sightseers.

"Can I get out?" Aaron asked before Daniel had brought the truck to a complete halt.

Maggie looked to Daniel, who nodded.

"Sure," he said, "but just stand next to the truck. I don't want you falling down the side of the mountain.

Aaron quickly climbed out of the vehicle and shut the door behind him. Instantly Maggie could feel the air in the truck cab begin to evaporate. As she met Daniel's gaze, her lungs felt as though they were laboring just to draw one breath, and her heart danced a jig as she met his gaze.

She didn't know what had come over her, but she knew for certain that if she didn't get ahold of her runaway emotions, she'd never last the whole weekend with this man. She'd collapse first.

"Uh, just what is it that we need to discuss?"

His gaze settled on her lips. "Where we're going to camp."

"Aren't the campsites down there?" She pointed toward the marina.

"The Bureau of Reclamations has built campsites all along the shoreline of this lake. But I thought Aaron might like something a little more primitive than cackling generators, loud radios and too many people to stir with a stick."

"Oh. Well, I'm not too keen on crowds, either," she admitted, albeit a little warily. "Just how primitive are you talking about?"

"No electricity or toilets. No campsites."

Maggie digested his words, then burst out with a short laugh. Was the man kidding? she wondered. But no, he looked as serious as a judge.

"Oh. Do you think we need to get *that*...primitive?"

To Maggie's surprise a little twist of a smile crossed his face, and she felt herself melting like snow in spring.

"We don't necessarily need to. I just thought it would make things more special for Aaron to see what real camping is like. I've brought plenty of kerosene lanterns and utensils to cook with over the fire. All you'll have to do is sit back and relax. Promise."

Maggie had never sat back and relaxed in her life. Not when there was any sort of work to be done. "But no toilets?"

"No. But there'll be plenty of trees and bushes."

In spite of her pink cheeks, she laughed. "Well, why not," she said. "It's just for a couple of days."

His eyes softened, and she thought she could see a glimpse of admiration in his dark-brown gaze. The idea made her feel good. Too good.

"I'm glad. I don't think you'll regret it. Why don't you call Aaron and we'll get on our way. The roads to where we're going are rough. It will take us a while."

As Daniel continued to drive them north across the Colorado border, she learned that this section of the lake rested on the Southern Ute Indian Reservation. She wondered if that fact made Daniel feel more at home.

Beneath her lowered lashes, she darted a look at his chiseled profile. There were so many things she would like to ask him. About his parents and his life growing up and about the joys and pains he'd experienced in his younger days. But he was a man of few words and he might take offense if she tried to pry anything from him.

Besides, Maggie told herself firmly, she didn't need to know every little thing about Daniel Redwing. He was just a man doing a kindness for Aaron and that was all.

Chapter Six

At Arboles they stopped at a convenience store for a bathroom break and to purchase a few last-minute articles Daniel thought they might need once they got into the wild. From there, he drove the truck onto a dirt road leading south into the mountains. The first mile or two was more or less like the dirt road leading into the T Bar K. There were a few holes and rocks, but basically it was smooth going. Unfortunately, the smoothness didn't last and the road turned into little more than a faint track leading around huge boulders and down washed-out gullies. In some areas they passed through thick forest, in others it opened up to arid meadows filled with sage and clumps of grass.

"Are you sure you know where you're going?"

Maggie asked, as the truck nosedived down a steep ravine. Holding on to the edge of the seat, she braced herself until they reached the bottom. There they bounced over loose rocks the size of basketballs, and Maggie had no way of preventing her shoulder from colliding with Daniel's. Thankfully, he seemed to expect her jostling. "We have to be miles away from civilization," she added.

Amused dimples marked his cheeks. "We are miles away from civilization. That's the whole point."

"Gee, Mom, this is neat," Aaron spoke up. His attention was all over the place as he searched the landscape for signs of wildlife. "I can't wait to set up camp."

Maggie looked down at her son. "You won't be afraid to stay out here in the wilderness tonight?"

Aaron shoved out his chest. "Gosh, no. Daniel will be with us."

As if that said it all, Maggie thought. Daniel's presence was obviously making Aaron feel secure, but as for her, each moment that passed with the man was making her more and more uneasy.

The three of them traveled for another half hour before the truck climbed down a short ravine and parked along a smooth, sandy beach.

Aaron jumped out of the truck immediately, and Maggie followed more slowly. Once she was standing on the ground, she looked around the secluded cove. One side was sheltered with high slabs of rock, the other with a thick forest of pine. The sand beneath her feet was soft and deep, almost as if they were on the ocean rather than a freshwater lake.

"What do you think?"

She jerked with surprise at the sound of Daniel's voice as he came up behind her. She hadn't heard him approach and he was definitely a man she needed to be braced for.

"It's beautiful. And so quiet." She glanced over her shoulder to see he was looking at her, and the warmth in his brown eyes made her pulse leap. "How did you know about this place?"

"My grandfather used to bring me here. We had good times fishing and camping together. But now he's too old to do much more than sit in his rocker and sleep." A rueful expression crossed his face. "But that's what happens when we get old."

Maggie nodded. "Yes. But getting old is a blessing. Believe me, I know."

Daniel realized she was referring to her husband and how his young life had ended so tragically. It wasn't what he wanted her to be thinking about. In fact, he wished that he could erase all that from her mind. He didn't want her thinking about the late Hugh Ketchum. Daniel wanted her thoughts to be on him. Which wasn't a smart thing. But he was a man, after all. And any normal, red-blooded man wanted to be the center of a woman's thoughts.

Clearing his throat, he lifted his gaze to the water lapping at the shore's edge. "We'd better get our camp set up," he suggested. "I'm sure Aaron wants to go fishing as soon as he can."

A few feet away, Aaron picked up on Daniel's words and trotted back to the two adults.

"Yeah! Can we go fishing now?" Aaron's eyes were dancing with excitement as he jumped up and down on the tips of his tennis shoes. "We can put up the tents and things later, can't we?"

With a shake of his head, Daniel took the boy by the shoulder. "Work first, play later. Having shelter is a serious matter. That's why we need to take care of the important things first. Okay?"

Aaron's head dipped a little with disappointment, but he didn't argue, and after a second or two he was grinning again. "Okay, Daniel, let's get to work!"

Daniel affectionately ruffled Aaron's hair, and Maggie was suddenly disturbed by the whole interaction. The two of them looked too right, too perfect together, she thought. Daniel wasn't Aaron's father. Nor would he ever be. What would that eventually mean to Aaron? she wondered. Especially when Daniel grew bored of their friendship and ended it?

Maggie tried not to think about any of those things as she helped Daniel and Aaron unload the tents and cooking equipment. This outing was only for two days. She didn't want to ruin it by dwelling on problems that might or might not happen.

Two hours later they had erected two tents, filled air mattresses for the beds and covered them all with bedclothes. Outside, on the tailgate of the truck, Daniel set up a little wooden cabinet for the food and cooking utensils. While Maggie dealt with arranging canned goods and cooking pots, Daniel and Aaron arranged a circle of large rocks, then went in search of dead limbs for a campfire.

From Maggie's experience with building fires, it took several attempts to get a stack of wood burning, but Daniel did it with one match and soon the smoking pine burst into flames. Once it was crackling merrily, he looked pointedly at Maggie.

"You could make coffee now." He was still squatting by the fire, and even though he was a few feet away from where she was sitting, she could see a teasing glint in his eyes.

Maggie laughed. "Is that an order or a suggestion, Brave Redwing?"

"Just a suggestion."

Rising to his full height, he turned his back to the fire. With his profile exposed to Maggie, she found her gaze traveling over his chiseled face and down the rock-hard length of his body.

If he'd lived back in the days when Native Americans lived solely off the land, he would have been a leader among his people, Maggie decided. He had that silent strength about him that made his presence much bigger than the next man and much too potent for her to ignore.

"All right. A pot of coffee would be nice," she agreed good-naturedly. She rose from the director's chair and began to gather the makings. "Does this mean I'm the appointed cook?"

"No. I invited you here for company, not to be the camp cook."

He was admitting that he wanted her company. The idea tinged her cheeks with a soft blush. Watch it, Maggie, she warned herself as she filled a coffee-pot with bottled water. You can't start melting each time the man looks at you or says something even remotely suggestive.

"Daniel, I've got my fishing line all ready," Aaron announced.

Maggie turned her head to see Aaron jump up from his seat on a nearby rock and carry his rod and reel over to Daniel.

He told Aaron, "Well, if that's the case, I'd better get mine and we'll head down to the lake."

A perplexed frown creased her forehead as she studied the two of them. "What about the coffee?" she asked. "I have it ready to put on the fire."

"Go ahead. I'll get Aaron settled and come back for it in a few minutes."

She nodded, and Daniel turned away to follow Aaron, who was trotting quickly toward the water.

Maggie turned her attention back to her task and soon she had a wire mesh rack placed over the burning wood and the coffee pot sitting over the low flames.

While she waited for the water and grounds to boil, she sat back in the canvas director's chair and turned her attention to the lake's edge. Off to the left of their little camp, next to a small willow tree, Daniel and Aaron were casting their fishing lines into the choppy water.

As she watched them, her gaze instinctively settled on Daniel. His wide stance and rippling shoulder muscles reminded her even more of his strong, powerfully built body, and before she realized what she was doing, she was daydreaming, fantasizing about how he would look undressed, how bronze and masculine he would appear against the white sheets on her bed.

The sound of liquid sizzling onto the flaming logs suddenly jerked Maggie out of her erotic reverie and she jumped to her feet to pull the pot away from the heat.

Cursing under her breath, she pulled off the lid and poured in a bit of cool water to settle the coffee grounds. She was embarrassed and angry with herself for allowing her thoughts to run away like that. It wasn't right for her to be lusting after a man when she'd loved Hugh so much.

But Hugh is gone. He'll never come back. He can't hold you, kiss you and make love to you like Daniel can.

The tiny voice inside her head was so real it scared her, and she was glad when she looked up and saw that Daniel was returning to camp. If she was having some sort of mental breakdown, at least he'd be around to take her for medical help!

"The coffee is ready," she told him. "In fact, it boiled over before I could get to it."

Shrugging, he glanced down at the fire. "The logs are still burning. It didn't hurt anything. But I should have shown you a trick to prevent that from happening."

The trick was not to daydream about having sex with you, Maggie thought. She took a deep breath and tried to swallow away the thickness in her throat.

"Oh? Is it an Indian trick?" she asked.

Amused grooves appeared on either side of his lips, and Maggie realized it was good to see him smile, to hear him chuckle. She liked to think she was making him happy for the moment. Which didn't make much sense. It wasn't her place to see that Daniel Redwing laughed or smiled. But she liked it when he did and she liked to think she had something to do with it.

"My grandfather taught me," he told her. "But whether he learned it from a Ute or a white man, I have no idea." He motioned toward the back of the truck. "Get some cups."

She fished two old melamine cups from the portable cupboard and turned back around to the fire. Daniel had squatted on his heels and had taken the lid off the coffeepot. She watched him place a small branch over the opening.

"This is what you do to keep the pot from boiling over," he told her.

Maggie laughed at the simple directive. "I don't believe it. A twig from a tree can't stop the coffee from spilling over the sides."

He cast her a smug smile. "Next time I'll make the coffee and show you."

In other words, he could back up his promises. Maggie wasn't sure if that announcement relieved her or not. Especially when she looked into his eyes and saw promises of kisses like the one he'd given her in the barn.

If only she could forget those few minutes. But she couldn't. Even now, after days had passed, the taste, the feel of him was still with her.

"Okay, I believe you." Close to his side, she crouched down on her heels and held the cups out to him. "Would you pour?"

His eyes lifted to hers and she watched, her heart pounding, as his nostrils flared and his fingers reached out and softly touched her cheek.

"You look at home out here in the wilderness," he said slowly, "with the sky behind you and the breeze blowing your hair. So very beautiful, Maggie."

Warm color filled her cheeks, and she looked down at the ground as reckless, forbidden sensations swarmed her whole body.

"Daniel, this time isn't for you and me," she felt the need to remind him.

"No. This trip is for Aaron. But that doesn't stop me from wanting you."

She had never met a man who said what he was thinking in such a straightforward manner. It shook her deeply to hear Daniel speak his mind. Especially when she was feeling the same way.

Maggie was still trying to think of the best way to reply when he leaned forward and closed the few inches between their lips. Shock and then intense pleasure flooded her senses as he kissed her with a yearning so soft, so sweet, it touched every part of her body.

Without even realizing it, she dropped the cups, and her hands clutched the folds at the front of his shirt. He moaned deep in his throat and brought his arms around her shoulders.

"Mom! Mom! Come look! I caught a fish. A big one!"

Aaron's excited shouts caused them both to jerk back as though each of them were touching fire.

Breathlessly, Maggie caught his gaze, and a tremor raced down her spine as she saw the smoldering desire in his brown eyes.

"I...think we'd better go see if your son has caught our dinner for tonight," he said huskily.

All Maggie could manage to do was nod, and he rose to his feet and offered a hand down to her. She took it, and the warm strength of his fingers enclosing hers was almost as intimate as the touch of his lips.

As they walked across the beach to where Aaron was fishing, Daniel continued to hold her hand. Splinters of pleasure dashed up her arm and danced a silly dance right between her breasts. In her head a joyous voice was shouting that she was wanted, that Daniel wanted to be connected to her. Not in a lecherous way, but in the basic way a man needs a woman.

Aaron looked away from his fishing line and over his shoulder long enough to see the two of them approaching and he began to shout all over again.

"Look behind me, Mom. It's a trout! A big trout! And I think I have another one on the line!" Twisting back around, her son began to reel in his line at a furious pace. "Oh boy, oh boy. This is great!"

Maggie was amazed to see that the trout Aaron had caught weighed at least three pounds. He'd simply allowed the fish to fall on the sand, so Daniel strung the trout on a stringer and staked it out in the cool water of the lake.

Maggie hugged Aaron's shoulders and praised him for his good fishing. "Skinny must have done a good job teaching you how to fish. I didn't know you were so good at it."

"I didn't, either," Aaron exclaimed.

Maggie and Daniel both laughed at his honesty and then Daniel said, "Skinny is the ranch hand. The old one. He taught Aaron about fishing?"

Maggie said, "Yes. I never knew anything about the sport. I was a horse girl. So I couldn't teach Aaron the first thing about a rod and reel or how to cast. Ross and Linc have fished, and both of them promised to take Aaron to the creek that runs through T Bar K property, but they never seem to have the time to do anything other than work the ranch."

"And now Ross has a wife," Daniel added. "That must take up even more of his time."

She smiled wryly. "Believe me, that's time Ross considers well spent."

"I'm sure," Daniel murmured.

Maggie glanced up at him and noticed his mouth was set in a grim line, which surprised her. Ross and Bella were perfect for each other. Their marriage was rock solid. Why would Daniel not be happy about that, she wondered. Or was it just the idea of marriage in general that put a sour look on his face?

Thankfully, she didn't have long to mull over the questions. Aaron pulled another trout from the water and was jumping up and down with excitement as Daniel took the fish off the hook.

"You'd better get your rod and reel and start fishing, too," Aaron said to Daniel. "They're really starting to bite!"

Daniel cast Maggie a fleeting smile before he walked over to the willow and picked up the fishing gear he'd stowed beside the tree.

Sighing, Maggie told herself it was a good thing that Aaron was dominating Daniel's attention. That kiss they'd shared by the fire was too deep to dismiss, and she could no longer pretend indifference. Not when her body was aching for him to hold her and make love to her.

Shaken by her thoughts, she headed back to the camp to fetch the coffee and try to collect her runaway senses.

Later that evening, Daniel built up the fire so there would be good coals to cook with. After that he cleaned the stringer of trout while Aaron tried his best to help.

Once the fish were ready to cook, he brought them over to the makeshift kitchen on the back of the truck and placed the trout on a large sheet of aluminum foil. Maggie stood by his side and watched him spread a layer of onion and lemon slices over the fish. After a hefty sprinkle of salt and pepper, he sealed up the foil and carried the shiny package over to the fire.

"Now whatcha goin' to do with the fish?" Aaron asked, who was sitting crossed legged on the ground, soaking up the warmth of the fire.

"Just watch," Daniel instructed.

With a small shovel, he raked the burning wood to one side to expose a bed of red-hot coals, then he placed the rack back over the fire and the package of fish on the rack.

"They'll have to cook about thirty or forty-five minutes before they'll be ready to eat," Daniel announced.

"Will it taste good?" Aaron wanted to know. "Mom fixes broiled salmon, but I don't like that stuff too much."

He made a face and shivered with distaste. Daniel laughed. "I promise you'll like this. I'm a good cook."

"Hmm, I'll be the judge of that, once this meal is over," Maggie teased.

He looked at her and she had the feeling that the faint smile she read on his face had nothing to do with cooking.

"I didn't say I was better at it than you," Daniel told her.

Maggie cleared her throat and looked at the odds and ends scattered across the tailgate. "Is there something I can do to help you?"

He walked back over to where she stood and picked up a can of pork and beans.

"Yeah. You can open these."

It wasn't much of a task, but Maggie was glad to do anything. If she didn't find something to keep her hands occupied, she was halfway afraid she was going to put them on him.

In the next half hour Daniel sliced peeled potatoes into a skillet filled with a small amount of oil, and fried them to a golden brown. She emptied the beans into a saucepan and placed them on the fire. Daniel spooned a heavy dose of chili powder into them and grinned at her.

"I like things spicy," he explained.

Maggie was beginning to see that. And she was also beginning to see that she shouldn't have come on this trip. She should have known that spending time with Daniel in a quiet family setting was the last thing she needed to do. It was making her crazy to touch him, be close to him. Even worse, it was making her think things that she had no right to think. Like how it might be if the three of them could always be together as they were at this moment.

Daniel's dinner was the most delicious meal Maggie could ever remember eating. The fish were succulent, the potatoes crisp on the outside and soft on the inside. Even the beans were tasty, and she ate until she was stuffed.

As for Aaron, he also made a pig of himself and he kept proudly reminding the two adults that he was the one who'd supplied the fish for their dinner. As Maggie watched her son stretch out by the warm fire, she could see he was in little-boy heaven. Daniel had made his dream come true and she would always be grateful to him for going to such lengths for Aaron's sake.

Once the sun slid behind the bank of rocks to the west, the night air began to cool dramatically. Maggie insisted that Aaron pull on a sweatshirt, and she covered her arms with a red corduroy shirt. Daniel built up the fire, and the three of them scooted closer to the flames.

"I brought a bag of marshmallows if anyone would like some," Maggie suggested.

"Too full," Daniel replied.

"I could eat some," Aaron spoke up. "I like to roast them until they're black."

Maggie got the marshmallows for her son. Earlier in the evening Daniel had cut a few willow sticks and sharpened the ends to use for roasting sticks. She gave one to Aaron and ordered him not to get up without laying the stick down first.

From the corner of her eye, she caught Daniel winking at her son and she looked at him with pursed lips.

"What's the matter? You think I'm being overprotective again?"

Daniel cast her a completely innocent look. "No. It's good for Aaron to know he has to be careful with a sharp object," he agreed. "Some parents just teach in a different way."

"Mom won't let me have a pocketknife either," Aaron mumbled as he shoved marshmallows on the end of the stick. "She says I might fall on it and jab it in me. Pooh. I'm smart enough to know I have to close it and keep it in my pocket while I'm running and playing."

"You might be smart enough," Maggie spoke up, "but you're not old enough. Not in my opinion."

Aaron didn't argue out loud. Instead he tried another tactic.

"You have a knife, don't you, Daniel?" Aaron questioned.

Maggie looked over as Daniel reached to a sheath on his belt and pulled out a long, shiny hunting knife.

"I have many knives," he said. "This hunting knife is the one I like to take camping. You can do lots of things with it—like clean trout."

"I'll bet your mother let you have a knife when you were littler than me," Aaron said with a careful eye toward Maggie.

"She didn't. But my grandfather, Joe SilverBear, gave me one and taught me how to use it. He also showed me how to catch fish with a bow and arrow."

Aaron forgot about his melting marshmallows. "Really? How old were you?"

Daniel shrugged. "Maybe ten. I can't remember exactly."

Aaron was suddenly a picture of attention. "What else did he teach you? How to hunt deer and elk with a bow and arrow?"

Daniel had a sip of coffee. "I was fortunate that I had my grandfather to teach me the old ways of our people. And hunting is one of the things a young Ute learns at an early age. With a bow and arrow and a rifle."

"Girls, too?" Aaron asked with disbelief.

Daniel grinned at his assumption. "No. Only the boys hunted for wild game. The girls learned to grow crops and make a shelter to live in."

"Sounds like you men couldn't have made it without the women," Maggie teased. "Grew the food, built the houses."

He looked at her, and in the flickering light of the fire, she could see his gaze was focused on her lips. Maggie took a deep breath and glanced away before he had a chance to see the longing that had been building inside her since early morning.

"We couldn't have made it," he admitted. "Not back before modern times. Today is different. Otherwise, I'd be in big trouble."

A mocking groan very nearly escaped Maggie's lips. If Daniel Redwing needed a woman to survive, he wouldn't be in the least bit of trouble. He was the strong, steady sort of man that drew women to him like the ocean to the shore. Knowing that, it was hard to understand why he wasn't married. Why had he never taken a wife, she wondered. Did he just not want to be around a woman for a permanent length of time? Or had he already been burned in love?

Maggie told herself that whatever was in Daniel's heart had nothing to do with her. Yet whenever he looked into her eyes and kissed her, Maggie wished she knew exactly what the man was thinking.

Chapter Seven

For the next half hour Daniel told Aaron several stories about some of the hunting trips that he and his grandfather, Joe SilverBear, had taken through the years.

Daniel also went on to explain how for over thirty years on the Ute Reservation, Joe had worked as a tribal policeman. Eventually he'd retired from the force, and his dedication to keeping law and order had inspired Daniel to be a lawman, too.

As Maggie listened to the stories Daniel told of his grandfather, she could see how much he adored and respected the old man. She also noticed the blatant absence of any words about his father. He'd told her his father had been killed, but surely he had his memories, she thought.

Just as Maggie was wondering about Daniel's father, Aaron spoke up and put her thoughts into a question of his own.

"What about your dad, Daniel? What did he teach you?"

Maggie watched in total dismay as Daniel's face suddenly went flat and devoid of emotion.

"My father taught me nothing," Daniel answered.

"How come?" Aaron prodded. "Was he dumb?"

Maggie gasped. "Aaron! That's an awful thing to say! Apologize immediately to Daniel or you're going to bed this instant!" she ordered hotly.

Ducking his head with shame, Aaron mumbled. "I'm sorry, Daniel. I didn't mean to say something bad about your daddy."

Without glancing at either of them, Daniel wiped a hand over his face and stared into the flames of the fire. "Forget it, Aaron, you didn't say anything bad, you were just asking a simple question." He glanced over at him. "Remember I told you that I didn't have a dad, either. He was killed in an accident, and before that happened, I wasn't around him much."

"Oh." Aaron looked contrite. "Well, you were lucky cause you had a good grandpa. I don't have any of those, either. They're both dead."

Daniel let out a sigh edged with regret, and Maggie wondered if the melancholy sound was due to Aaron's loss or his own.

"Yes, Joe SilverBear is someone I love a lot. He took me to my first bear dance," Daniel stated. "And I still try to attend the festival whenever I have the chance."

Intrigued, Maggie asked, "What is a bear dance? You wrestle bears or something?"

To her relief the somber look on Daniel's face lifted and he chuckled aloud while across the way Aaron let out an embarrassed groan.

"Aw, Mom, you know Daniel is smart enough to know not to wrestle a bear. He'd get killed!"

Still chuckling, Daniel said, "Thanks for your confidence in my intelligence, Aaron."

"Girls!" Aaron said with disdain. "They're not too brainy about some things. Did you know that, Daniel? There's a girl who sits behind me in school and she's always popping me in the head with her pencil. She thinks it's funny."

"She's only doing that because she likes you and wants you to say something to her," Daniel told him. "And you'd better remember that your mother is a very smart woman. You should always respect her intelligence."

Aaron crammed the blackened marshmallows into his mouth and spoke around them. "Mom is the greatest. She knows that."

Maggie rolled her eyes and smiled at her son's buttery comment. To Daniel she said, "So tell us about the bear dance. What is it? A ritual of the Utes?"

Nodding, Daniel leaned forward and picked up a

nearby stick. As he poked the fire, he said, "It happens every spring because everyone is glad that winter is finally over. The men and women gather for a four-day festival. A corral is built, and inside the corral they all sing and dance in honor of the bear."

Aaron scooted around the fire and rested his chin on Daniel's knee. "Why do they do that?" he asked. "Bears are killers."

"Yes. But they are also smart survivors. And there is a story as to why the Utes do the bear dance every year. Do you want to hear it?"

"Tell us! Tell us!" Aaron urged.

Daniel gently stroked his hand over Aaron's brown hair, and as Maggie looked on, her heart squeezed with bittersweet emotions. For years she'd wished that Aaron could have a father, a man who would love and guide him as his own. But to give her son that gift would mean she would have to marry again. So far she'd refused to even consider the idea. But Daniel was making her think of the prospect more and more. Was he making her crazy? Daniel was a confirmed bachelor, and she was a widow. There could never be anything permanent between them.

"Well...many, many years ago," Daniel began, "two Ute brothers went out hunting in the mountains. And they hunted until they were very tired, so they decided to lie down to rest. While they were resting, one of the brothers noticed a bear standing upright by a tree. He was dancing on his hind legs and making a noise as he clawed at the tree.

"The other brother ignored the bear and went on with his hunting, but his brother stayed and continued to watch. The bear taught the young brave to do the same dance and to sing the song. He told him to return to his people and to teach them the dance and songs of the bear so that they could show their respect for the bear spirit."

Aaron straightened away from Daniel's knee. "And if you respect the bear it makes you strong," Aaron said, repeating what Daniel had told him earlier in the day.

Daniel was surprised that the boy had remembered his comment about the bear spirit, and it struck him that he needed to be careful about everything he said to Aaron. The child was at a very impressionable age and obviously had a bit of hero worship for him. Perhaps because he was a deputy, Daniel thought. Or maybe it was simply because he was a man and could teach him about grown-up things.

"Right," Daniel told him.

"Is that all there is to the celebration?" Maggie asked. "Dancing and singing?"

Daniel looked at her beautiful face in the firelight, and his heart went as soft as one of Aaron's melted marshmallows. She was like a white princess who'd chosen to travel into the wilderness with an Indian brave. The fanciful idea swelled his heart like nothing ever had, and he realized after this time spent with her, it was going to be very difficult to put her out of his life.

"No. Not at all. At the bear dance celebration there is all sorts of food to eat and everyone visits and swaps stories. And there is a special custom on the final day of the festivities. The men and women wear a feather into the corral, and when they leave at the end of the day, they leave the feather on a cedar tree, which will always be located at the east entrance of the corral."

"What does that do?" Aaron spoke up before Maggie had a chance.

Daniel gave the boy a brief smile, then cut his eyes toward Maggie. "Leaving the feather behind on the tree means that you're leaving your troubles behind you and starting your life anew."

Maggie sighed. "That's so beautiful, Daniel."

Daniel reached over and took her by the hand. "Sometimes we all need to do that, Maggie. Are you ready to leave your feather on the cedar tree?"

Sweet, painful emotions clogged her throat as she looked at him and tried to figure the real meaning of his question. Was he asking her to forget all the pain she'd endured over Hugh and start her life over with him?

Shaken by the thought, Maggie's gaze slipped to the dark ground as she pulled her hand from his.

After a moment she said in a husky voice. "I wish things were that simple."

"So do I," she heard him murmur.

The three of them remained by the campfire for another half hour and by then Aaron's chin kept hitting his chest as the boy struggled to stay awake. Maggie didn't have the heart to tell him to go to the tent and get in bed. Instead she waited until he'd fallen completely asleep before she rose from her chair.

"I think Aaron is down for the count. I'd better get him in bed before he catches cold," she told Daniel.

She was bending down to gather her son into her arms when she felt Daniel's hand on her shoulder.

"He's too heavy for you," he said as he urged her to one side. "Let me do it."

Aaron was a solidly built boy, so Maggie was relieved to step aside and turn the task over to Daniel. He lifted the child's weight effortlessly into his arms and carried him over to the two domed tents they had erected earlier in the day. The shelters were positioned about ten feet away from the fire and some five feet away from each other. At Maggie's tent Daniel waited while she unzipped the flap.

Inside the cozy room, Daniel placed the sleeping boy on one of the inflated mattresses. "Are you going to undress him?" he asked quietly.

Maggie shook her head. "I'll just take his shoes and jeans off. He'll be warm enough under the covers."

Along with Daniel's blankets, she'd brought a few of her own just in case they might be needed. Since the night was very cool, she fetched a couple of them from a duffle bag.

After hastily removing Aaron's shoes and jeans, she covered him with several blankets and tucked them carefully around him. Once she was finished, she glanced up to see Daniel watching her closely, and like before when he'd talked about his father, his expression was a closed enigma.

"Aaron is very lucky that his mother loves him so much," he whispered.

His unexpected comment caused her throat to thicken with emotion. Her voice was husky as she said, "No. I am the lucky one to have a son."

He didn't say anything to that, and after a moment he gave Aaron one last glance and slipped from the tent. Maggie quickly followed.

Outside the tent, the night had grown darker, the stars brighter. A cool breeze was blowing off the lake. Maggie rubbed her arms as she went to stand with her back to the fire.

Daniel tagged along behind her and for a long time the two of them simply stood there together, quietly absorbing the night. For several miles in any direction there wasn't another human. Maggie doubted very many regular folks ever ventured back this far into the wilderness. The way was arduous and most people didn't like to rough it to this extent.

"Sorry you came?" he asked.

His voice surprised her and her head jerked around toward his. "Why, no. Why do you ask?"

He shrugged nonchalantly. "Just wondered. I, uh, haven't known any women who would do this sort of thing. You surprise me, Maggie Ketchum."

He was complimenting her again, and his words flowed through her like a drink of warm, pleasing wine. "This isn't a hardship, Daniel. I love the outdoors. When I was a small girl I spent my days outside with my horses."

His brow lifted slightly. "Where was this?"

"Denver. My dad was in real estate, in a big way. My parents were—"

"Rich," he finished before she could.

Maggie's face warmed at the word. She didn't want him to get the idea that she'd ever been a snob. As far as she was concerned she'd never been interested in money. True, she'd married into a wealthy family, but she hadn't needed or wanted Hugh's money. And even now she lived modestly in the same small ranch house she'd shared with him.

"Well, my parents never wanted for money. Thanks to my father's hard work."

"Aaron said his grandfathers are dead. I was acquainted with Tucker. What happened to your father?"

Maggie's expression was suddenly regretful. "I don't know, really. Too much work and mental stress, I suppose. He was in his late fifties when his heart gave out."

"That's too bad. It would have been much better for you to still have him around than the money he provided."

Dear God, how absolutely right this man was, she thought.

"That's very true, Daniel. I miss him deeply. And the irony of it now is that—" She paused and shook her head. "I shouldn't be saying any of this—"

"This what?" he urged. "Why shouldn't you be saying it? There's no one here but the two of us. And I don't repeat what I've been told in confidence."

"I'm not worried about you repeating anything. I just shouldn't be talking about my family in—such a way." Her lips twisted to a bitter slant. "But like you said, who would ever know. Certainly not my mother. It's a rare occasion when I hear from her."

Daniel appeared very surprised over this admission, and he peered at her closely. "You don't get along with your mother?"

Maggie shook her head. "I'm afraid not. She—well, even when I was a child, we never got along. I think she always resented the fact that my father and I were so close." She glanced up at him, and for a moment a brief smile erased the line in the middle of her forehead. "My father and I shared the same deep love of horses, and by the time I was thirteen I was competing in cutting-horse competitions. We traveled all over the country to different shows and horse sales."

"And your mother, did she go along on these trips?" he asked sagely.

Maggie's head shook with regret. "No. Mother was more of a fashion plate. She didn't like anything to do with the outdoors. Her thing was to socialize and give parties for my father's business partners. She also enjoyed planning charity functions and fund-raisers for local politicians. She wouldn't get within twenty feet of a horse, and she resented the fact that Daddy had gotten me interested in a 'man's sport' as she called it."

"So this is why you're not in touch with her now?"

Maggie looked away from him and shrugged a second time. "No. The straw that broke the camel's back was when she remarried. Her husband wanted nothing to do with Aaron or me, nor did he want us in Mother's life. It was obvious he was afraid she would will all of the money she'd gotten from Daddy to us, rather than him. I tried to make her see what a leech he was, but she told me to get out and never come back. So I haven't," she added firmly, then glanced up at him. "I never wanted Daddy's money, Daniel. For heaven's sake, Hugh left me plenty. All I wanted from her was—well, for us to be a family."

"I'm sorry, Maggie."

She cast him a wry smile. "So now you're probably thinking I was spoiled by my father."

He shrugged. "Not really. You don't come across to me as a pampered woman. And I think it's great that the two of you were so close."

It was absolutely silly how good his comment made her feel. His opinion of her shouldn't matter at all. But in fact it was beginning to mean everything. And that admission caused a thread of fear to wind around her heart.

"Well, I'm not going to deny that I had it easy while I was growing up. Daddy was generous about buying me any horse I wanted. And since I fell in love with every one of them I laid eyes on, that turned out to be a good many."

The faint smile on his face said that he understood. "I'm not surprised. There's something about girls and horses."

She laughed and then her expression sobered as she looked at him.

"Daniel, I'm so sorry about Aaron saying what he did about your father. He didn't mean to be disrespectful. I hope it didn't hurt your feelings."

A mocking sound erupted from deep in his throat. "Hardly, Maggie. Aaron was just being a normal kid. Children say exactly what they think."

She turned so that she was facing the fire and as she gazed down at the flames, she ventured to say, "I got the feeling that you didn't want to talk about your father."

Daniel followed her example and turned to face the fire also. "No. He's not a pleasant subject."

"Would it make you angry if I asked why?"

He let out a long breath, then lifted his gaze up from the flames and stared into the shadows surrounding their small camp.

"Why do you want to know?"

Feeling awkward now, she shrugged. "Girls don't just have love affairs with horses, they also have problems with nosiness."

He grunted with amusement and then fell silent. Long minutes passed without any sounds except for the wind in the cedars, the soft lapping of the water and the crackle of the campfire.

Maggie had already decided he was going to ignore her question completely when he started to speak again.

"You're right, Maggie. I don't like to talk about my father. He brought shame to my mother and me, to our family. He was no good."

Regret for him raced through her and left a knot in the pit of her stomach. "You told Aaron that you didn't really know him. Was that true?"

Daniel shrugged. "In a sense. I was probably Aaron's age when Robert Redwing finally left our home. By then I'd seen enough to make me wish he wasn't my father. He loved the 'firewater' as he always called it. He'd get tanked up most every day and when he did, he'd get mean with my mother and me. When he was sober, he was a sullen, depressed man who wanted to blame his problems on everyone but himself. I was glad when he finally left us."

Dear Lord, how awful, she thought as her heart ached for what he must have gone through as a child.

"What about your mother? Was she glad he left, too?"

Daniel rubbed a hand through his thick, black hair. "I've often wondered about that. My mother, Pelipa, is not a woman who speaks her feelings to others. And down through the years, she hasn't mentioned Robert very often. As far as I'm concerned, she was much better off without him. But Pelipa was raised in the old ways. To her, a wife's duty is to respect and devote herself to her husband, no matter what. I think she's always thought of herself as a failure because her husband left her—that it was her fault because she should have made him happier." He paused and made a bitter, mocking sound. "No one could have made that man happy."

So Daniel hadn't had a normal family upbringing, she thought sadly. And thinking on it, she was actually amazed that he'd turned out to be such a good, steadfast man.

"What about your mother now? Did she ever remarry?"

He shot her a rueful look. "We were living in Bloomfield at the time the bastard took off. After that, we moved back to the reservation in Colorado, and until this day my mother hasn't stepped foot off it. The outside world is a harsh place to her. At least the reservation makes her feel safe. My mother will never remarry or look at another man. Robert Redwing ruined her chances for happiness."

"How did he get killed? Do you know?"

"A relative of Robert's who lived in Arizona gave us a sketchy account. Something about him driving a truck through a guardrail and landing upside down in an arroyo. Before that he'd been in and out of the Arizona State Penitentiary for theft."

Maggie slowly shook her head. "I'm so sorry, Daniel. I know that sounds stupid to be saying such a thing to you now. But I truly mean it. I wish your young life had been different—better."

She could hear him breathe deeply, and when he looked at her, Maggie could see he was grateful that she understood and wasn't condemning him for his father's shortcomings.

"I wished it had been, too," he said quietly. "But it can't be changed now. I can only look forward. Just as you should only look forward."

Maggie understood what he was trying to tell her. And she knew he was right. She needed to let go of the past, let go of Hugh's ghost, but she'd clung to it for so many years now that it was like a child's safety blanket. She was afraid if she ever let go, the pain would come crashing back in.

They stood there in silence for a few moments, both of them soaking up the relaxing heat of the fire. Maggie was acutely aware that there was only an inch or two separating their arms, and the idea of stepping closer and touching him kept going round and round in her mind like an erotic mantra she couldn't shut out.

"I, uh, think I'd better make a bathroom trip and get ready for bed," she finally said. "Do you have a flashlight I can use?"

"I'll get it for you," he told her.

Maggie followed him to the truck where he dug the light from a stack of things on the front seat. Thankfully, she had clean tissue in her jeans pocket. It would be more than embarrassing to ask him for something so personal.

"Would you like me to go with you?" he asked as he shut the door on the truck and turned back to her.

Maggie stared at him wide-eyed. "Why no! I can make it by myself."

Even though it was darker where they were now

standing, she could see that he was frowning impatiently at her.

"I didn't mean it like that," he said. "I can stay away from you and keep my back turned. You might feel safer."

A wolf, a bear or even a mountain lion couldn't frighten her as much as the feelings she was having for Daniel. Even when she was much younger and with Hugh, she'd never felt so gripped with physical need, and that both shocked and frightened her.

"N-no, I'll be fine," she assured him, and though she was trying her best not to sound nervous, she knew she sounded like a stuttering schoolgirl.

"I'll wait for you by the fire," he said.

All she could do was nod and then she scampered off into the dark woods, knowing the real threat to her safety was behind her.

A few minutes later she returned to camp and went to the tailgate of the pickup where Daniel had set up a plastic washbasin, soap and water.

As she washed her hands, he asked, "Would you like me to heat you a bucket of water to wash with?"

Maggie tossed handfuls of cold water onto her face and wiped it off with a towel.

"There's no need for all that trouble," she told him. "I'm just cleaning my face and hands. The rest of me can wait until I get back to civilization."

Jamming her hands in the back pockets of her jeans, she walked over to the fire. "I guess I'll go to bed now," she announced.

His brows rose as he glanced at his wristwatch. "It's only eight o'clock. Do you usually go to bed this early?"

Maggie felt her cheeks suddenly flood with embarrassed heat, and she could only hope the orange glow from the flames was camouflaging the telltale color on her face.

"No. But out here—this is different."

He turned his head, and she could feel his dark gaze boring into her. "We'll only be here for tonight. You should enjoy it instead of trying to run away from me."

Maggie's jaw dropped as she looked up at him. His chiseled profile was etched with firelight and she could easily imagine him as he might have been if he'd lived when the Utes still roamed free and wild over the San Juan Mountains. He'd be dressed in tanned leather and his black hair would rest long and straight upon his shoulders. His language would be Shoshone, but the glint of desire in his eyes would be the same dangerous light she was seeing now.

"Run away?" She sputtered with nervous laughter. "Do I look like I'm trying to run away?"

Daniel studied her face. "You want to hide in your bed."

Pressing her lips together, she drew in a long, shaky breath. "For your information, I'm tired. I'm not used to being in the outdoors this much. And the trip up here was tiring."

Mocking amusement dented both of his cheeks. "I don't believe you're a bit tired. You don't look it."

She cleared her throat as nervousness overtook her. "You seemed to know a lot about me all of a sudden."

He moved closer, and her breathing grew short and rapid as he reached out and placed his hand around her upper arm.

"Every minute I'm learning more," he murmured.

She groaned with misgivings. "Daniel, please...we didn't come out here for...this."

"This? I'm just touching your arm."

Turning ever so slightly, Maggie placed her palms against his chest. "That's a start to something I—"

She couldn't continue. Every beat of her heart was pumping hot desire through her veins.

His hands began to move up and down her arms in a warm, seductive way. "Maggie, I want you. I've wanted you ever since we kissed that night after we brought Aaron home from the mountains. If that's bad or wrong, I can't help it."

Squeezing her eyes shut, she swallowed at the husky knot in her throat. It would be stupid of her to try to hide her feelings, she thought, especially when she wanted, needed him so much.

Her eyes dropped to the middle of his chest where her fingers unwittingly plucked at the fabric of his shirt. "I...want you, too, Daniel. But we can't have what we want. It wouldn't be—"

"Right?" he finished for her. "Why? Because I'm Ute?"

"No! That's an awful thing to say."

Lifting his hand to her face, he cupped his palm

against her cheek. "What am I supposed to think? You're a single woman, free from commitment. Why would it be wrong for you to make love to me?"

Make love to him. Yes. That's exactly what Maggie wanted to do. What she'd wanted to do for weeks now. "I don't know why it would be wrong—it just would."

She could see he was fighting with himself as much as he was with her way of thinking. "Maybe." He said. "But right now, tonight, I don't care."

He didn't wait for her to reply. The tug of his hands brought her straight into his arms. Her head fell back, and Daniel took advantage by closing his mouth over hers.

The moment she tasted his lips, Maggie realized there was no turning away. The hunger deep inside her had been growing and building for days now. She couldn't ignore it or deny it…no matter the consequences.

Rising up on tiptoe, she slid her hands up his shoulders and circled her arms around his neck.

Maggie's welcoming response caused a groan to purr deep in Daniel's throat, and his hands slid to her buttocks to pull her tight against his swelling manhood. Finally, when they were both desperate for air, he broke the contact of their lips and whispered in a gravelly voice against the side of her neck.

"I want you, Maggie. Very much. Feel me. Feel what you're doing to me." He unwound one of her arms from his neck and placed her hand on the fly of his pants.

If he expected her to be shocked by the bulge beneath the heavy denim of his jeans, she wasn't. Not if he was feeling anything like she was at this moment. Her own body was aching desperately, and she wondered how this one man could have so quickly resurrected something that had been dead inside her for many years.

Pressing her cheek against his chest, she murmured, "I want you, too, Daniel. So very much."

He didn't waste time in saying more. He didn't want to give her the chance to second guess what they were about to do. In his mind he had no choice. Tomorrow might bring regrets. But tonight, for the first time in his life, he was going to follow the calling in his heart.

Chapter Eight

Bending, he swept her up in his arms and carried her to his tent. Inside the small enclosure, he laid her on the smooth mattress, then began to remove his shirt.

Once it was out of the way, he lay down next to her and drew her into his arms. She was shivering, and as she clung to his shoulders, he reached down and pulled a blanket up over the two of them.

"Better?" he asked as she rested her head in the hollow of his shoulder.

"I'm...not cold," she answered. "I guess I'm...a little nervous. I don't have to tell you that it's been a long time since—well, you know."

Tilting his head downward, he placed his lips against the crown of her curly hair. "Not since Hugh?"

She shook her head. "I've never wanted anyone like this. I've never felt this way—ever."

The glow of the nearby fire illuminated the interior of the tent with dim yellow light. Maggie tilted her head back to search out the handsome lines of his face.

"I'm glad," he said simply. "Because I've never felt like this, either."

It wasn't something he'd wanted to admit to her. He wanted to keep this need, this connection to her purely physical. But that idea had flown away the moment his lips had touched hers. Something about Maggie made his head and his heart merge in an all-too-vulnerable way.

To push the worry away, Daniel moved his head forward and began to kiss her again. The warm response of her lips heated his blood until the pleasure exploding in his body overcame the trouble in his mind.

Soft kisses turned hungry, and soon he was peeling away the two shirts she was wearing, her blue jeans and hiking boots. When he'd finally stripped her down to a scanty pair of panties and a bra, he turned to remove the rest of his own clothing.

As he lay down next to her on the makeshift bed, Maggie allowed her gaze to roam over his perfect body. He was lean in all the right places, while the rest of him was hard muscle.

She reached for him at the same time he reached for her, and his bronze skin was hot and smooth beneath her fingers. Maggie buried her face into the crook of his shoulder and allowed her hands to explore his back, his ribs and the rock-hard muscles of his stomach.

His lips found the side of her neck and he nibbled his way softly upward until he pulled the lobe of her ear into his mouth and bit down with teasing pressure.

Maggie moaned with pleasure and snuggled closer to the hard heat of his body.

"Will Aaron wake up?" he whispered the question even as his hands worked to undo the clasp between her breasts holding together the two pieces of fabric.

"No. Once he's asleep, he goes out like a rock," Maggie told him.

"I've tied the zipper to our door closed. Just in case," he assured her.

Their brief words caused a moment of sanity to enter her brain, and she looked at him with a measure of hesitation. "Are we—is this really what we want, Daniel?"

Groaning deep in his throat, he pushed the lace away from her breasts. "A long time ago when I had just grown into manhood, my grandfather told me that I would someday make love to a woman with fiery hair and she would change me. I never thought of his words again—until tonight, as we stood by the fire."

Shaken by the old Indian's prophecy, Maggie searched his face. "How did he know such a thing?" she asked in a surprised tone.

Daniel's fingers threaded themselves through the silky curls at the side of her face. "He said he saw us one morning as he watched the sunrise. He said we were naked and entwined as one."

"Oh, no." She groaned with embarrassment and turned her face away from his.

"Maggie, why does that cause you shame? It made him very happy."

Her fingers traced lazy circles upon his chest. "He talked to you about—sexual things?"

The surprise in her voice put a faint smile on Daniel's face. "He talked to me about everything that had to do with the earth and the spirits beyond."

She thought about the whole thing for a few moments, and then she suggested, "Maybe you've already made love to a fiery-haired woman."

His response was nothing like she expected. He began to laugh, almost loudly, and she pushed the upper part of her body away from his to stare at him.

"Is that supposed to be funny?" she asked.

"I have never made love to a white woman, period. And a few weeks ago, if someone had told me that I would have Maggie Ketchum in my bed tonight, I would have considered him crazy."

"Why?" She wanted to know.

He made another grunt of amusement. "Because you are the rich princess on Ketchum Mountain. Women like you don't rub shoulders or anything else with a Ute."

Anger slashed through her and she pressed her palm over his lips so that he couldn't speak. "Do you think I am really that way? That I'm prejudiced? That I'm just a money person? Dear Lord, if you do, then I shouldn't be here in this tent with you!"

Drawing her hand from his mouth, he brought his lips close to hers. "Shh! I didn't say I thought that now. I'm only telling you how I felt before I really got to know you. And now every time I look at you I want you. I don't care if you are a Ketchum or a rich, white woman," he said fiercely.

The urgency in his voice pierced something deep within her, and with a tiny groan she closed the distance between their lips and clutched her arms tightly around him.

"No! It doesn't matter. Nothing matters," she whispered once their kiss ended. "Except that you love me."

With his hand upon her brow, he tilted her head and began to kiss the exposed curve of her throat. "My little night bird, let me spread your wings," he murmured thickly.

Her head swimming, Maggie clutched his strong shoulders as his mouth made a wet descent down her throat and even lower to the soft spot between her breasts. There he laved her satiny skin with his tongue, while his fingers teased both nipples into hard buds.

The tug of his fingers and the intimate warmth of his tongue were enough to send her writhing with pleasure, and she moaned until he finally moved his mouth to her breast and began to suckle the nipple.

Intense pleasure shot through her like a flaming arrow, and her hand made a downward search for his manhood. As her fingers closed around his heated shaft, she heard him moan with pleasure, felt his teeth tighten upon the center of her breast.

"Daniel. Daniel."

His name was a whispered plea from Maggie's lips and he lifted his head and connected his mouth to hers. Nipping her lower lip with his teeth, he brought his hand between her thighs and pressed his palm against the moist ache.

Whimpering with need, Maggie stroked him, urged him to join their bodies. Desire consumed her and erased everything from her thoughts except him. She scarcely knew when he removed her panties, her hands were too busy searching out every hard muscle, every smooth contour of his body. Her lips were too distracted by the tug and pull of his teeth, the teasing touch of his tongue.

"Maggie," he finally whispered against her throat. "I don't have any protection. Do you?"

For a moment her mind was too drunk to realize what he'd asked, and then, as the question sank in, she pulled her head back and looked into his face.

"After all these years? I've never needed it."

Even though she kept her arms wrapped firmly around him, he groaned. "Do you...want to end this?" he asked, his voice hoarse with need.

Did she? No! It was no longer a choice. She had to have this man. He'd opened her eyes and her heart. He'd made her body throb back to life. She couldn't turn away from that now.

"No."

He drew in several deep, shuddering breaths as he tried to maintain control over his body.

"What if you get pregnant?"

For some reason she couldn't begin to fathom, the question didn't scare her. Nor did the idea of having his baby. Dear Lord, what was happening to her? Was she falling in love with this man?

"If that happens, it's meant to be," she said simply.

She heard the sharp, sudden intake of his breath, and for several seconds she thought he was going to turn away from her, to tell her that he was a no-strings, take-no-chances kind of man.

But he didn't turn away. Instead his fingers began to stroke her cheek, and her heart commenced to melt, to throb with an emotion so tender she thought it might rip her apart.

"My little Maggie. Oh yes, this was meant to be. Just as my grandfather predicted."

As his words faded away, his knee separated her thighs, his mouth returned to hers. Maggie shifted her body to receive him and, as he slowly entered her, tears of emotion slid from the corners of her eyes.

Daniel bent his head to kiss away the tracks of moisture on her cheeks. "Am I hurting you?" he asked urgently.

Maggie's head shook back and forth. "No. I don't know. Oh, just make love to me, Daniel," she pleaded.

She didn't have to ask him again. His body began to move inside hers, and she lifted her hips to meet his eager thrust.

In a matter of moments Maggie, overtaken with sensations, clung to him tightly, afraid to let go, afraid both of them would float away on a cloud.

The air inside the small tent grew as hot as their bodies, and soon Maggie's hair and skin were damp with sweat. Beneath her hands, Daniel's torso was also slick. And as he worked to assuage both of their needs, a drop of his salty perspiration touched her lips.

It wasn't long before Maggie felt the center of her being coiling tighter and tighter, until she was certain she would break apart. Finally, when the loop inside her snapped, she cried out as a million stars showered down on her.

Maggie's sobs of pleasure spurred Daniel to reach for that same corner of the sky, and soon after, his body jerked then shuddered as his release spilled inside of her.

When Maggie finally caught her breath and recognized that she was still alive, she could feel Daniel's soft, warm breath brushing the back of her neck, and feel his leg thrown possessively over hers. His hand was stroking the curve of her hip, and she closed her eyes to the pure pleasure of being his lover.

Lifting his hand to her lips, she kissed the back of it. "Tell me about Joe SilverBear," she murmured.

A chuckle rumbled inside his chest. "I make love to a woman and she wants to talk about my grandfather."

Smiling in the darkness, Maggie turned in his arms and snuggled her face against his shoulder. "We don't need to talk about what we just did. It was perfect. Don't you think?"

Closing his eyes, Daniel stroked her hair and the ridges of her spine. Making love to Maggie was unlike anything he'd ever experienced. His head was still reeling, and as far as he was concerned, to call their union perfect was not nearly a great enough description.

"It was beautiful, Maggie. More beautiful than I can tell you."

Her soft fingers began to draw absent patterns across his belly, and Daniel felt the faint flutter of desire tease his loins all over again.

Tilting her head backward, she kissed his chin, his jaw and finally the hollow beneath his cheekbone. As her fingers brushed through his thick, damp hair, she said, "I thought I would feel like a tart if I made love to another man. But I don't feel that way at all."

There was a wondrous tone threading through her words that touched Daniel and caused him to close his eyes and clench his teeth at the soft, sweet emotions clawing at his heart. He didn't want to give in to those feelings. He couldn't give in to them. He wasn't cut out to be a husband, a father. He would make a mess of their lives, just as Robert Redwing had made a mess of his and Pelipa's.

Daniel had believed he would feel relief once he and Maggie made love. But relief was not among the commotion going on inside him.

"A tart, huh? My grandfather *saw* you as a special lady."

Once again Maggie felt an eerie chill creep along her spine, and she reached for the cover at their feet.

"The fire is dying," she reasoned as she drew the blanket over his shoulder.

He drew her closer and she sighed as his chin came to rest on the top of her head.

"Do you really want to hear about Joe SilverBear?"

"Of course. He's your grandfather. How old is he?"

"Eighty-two."

Maggie was surprised. "That old? He's old enough to be your great-grandfather."

"Yes. Pelipa was past forty when she gave birth to me. Before that, she was barren. And she believed my father became an alcoholic because she could only give him one child," he said with faint mockery. "I thank God my grandfather was around to keep her from falling apart when Robert left."

"Joe SilverBear sounds like a strong man."

"He is. Both mentally and physically. And a part of me has always wanted to be like him. Joe inspired me to be a lawman and wanted me to work for the tribal police. He never wanted to leave the reservation and he believed that I shouldn't want to leave it either. I don't think he's ever quite forgiven me for that," he said pensively.

"Does he still live on the reservation in Colorado?"

"Yes. He draws a retirement pension for all those years he served as a tribal policeman. It's not much, but he has everything he wants. His house sits across a small mesa from my mother. She likes to say she is taking care of him, but I think it's always been the other way around."

Maggie went quiet for a few moments and then she mused aloud, "I wonder why he saw you making love to me—or some woman with red hair?"

Daniel's hands gently caressed her back. "Down through the years Joe has *seen* lots of things. I used to think he must drink mescal and have hallucinations. But my grandfather doesn't drink anything alcoholic. So it has to be some sort of gift—or cross to bear. Whichever way you want to look at it."

"Hmm. Did he ever say anything about us doing it more than once?" Maggie asked playfully.

Chuckling, Daniel eased her onto her back and cupped both hands around her breasts. "I don't know. I'll ask him someday. Just to see if he's right."

It was the wee hours of the morning before Maggie finally got dressed and crossed the short distance to her own tent. Daniel had been reluctant to let her leave the cozy warmth of his arms. But she'd argued that she couldn't allow Aaron to wake and find her in his tent. And thankfully Daniel had agreed.

Inside the dome structure, she found Aaron fast asleep under his blankets. She tucked the cover back around his shoulders, then sat down to remove her hiking boots.

Since the air had grown very cool in the early-morning hours, Maggie didn't bother to take off her clothing before she slipped into bed. Besides, she was too exhausted to deal with putting on pajamas. Every muscle, every nerve in her body was screaming for rest. And she only wished her mind would do the same. But it was racing, jumping in leaps and bounds from Daniel's lovemaking to the future. What was it all going to mean? she wondered.

Nothing. It can't mean anything.

The little voice shattered every hope in her heart, but she realized she had to stop and listen to it. Even if she was brave enough to make a life with another man, Daniel had issues of his own. He obviously wanted her physically. But that didn't mean he wanted to *love* her. Or that he *could* love her.

Her hand slid down her belly and rested in the hollow where her womb lay. Dear God, they could have made a baby, she thought. But she'd understood that risk before they'd taken it. And even now a tiny part of her soared with joy at the idea of having Daniel's baby, at the idea that her lonely life was finally going to change.

But she'd had one son and was now raising him without a father. Did she really want to put herself in a position for that to happen again?

Squeezing her eyes shut, she willed her mind not to think of the future. But after a few minutes she realized she couldn't stop it, and she fell asleep with the image of Daniel's face lying next to hers.

In the morning Daniel cooked a hearty breakfast of bacon and eggs and skillet toast. Normally, on the days he headed off to school, Aaron picked at a bowl of cereal, but this morning he scraped his plate clean and asked for seconds. Maggie was also hungrier than usual, and she was grateful for the hot food and coffee that Daniel had prepared for them.

After the leisurely meal, Maggie and Daniel took Aaron on a long hike over the rocks and hills that surrounded the camping area. Her son skipped and raced and explored everything around him with wondrous excitement.

As for Maggie, she walked quietly at Daniel's side. Every now and then the two of them would exchange heavy, silent glances and more than once he reached out and took her by the hand.

The sweet, simple touch stirred Maggie just as much as their hot, urgent lovemaking, and as they walked along, she kept trying to convince herself that she wasn't falling in love with him. But deep down she realized she couldn't fool herself.

Maggie wasn't just falling for Daniel. She was tumbling. Face forward, hard and fast. And the thing that scared her the most was that she couldn't see any way to stop the crash.

Chapter Nine

Even though they packed up and left the campsite shortly after lunch, it was late in the evening when they finally arrived back at the ranch.

Skinny was parked in front of the yard fence. Apparently he'd just driven up the mountain to feed the horses for Aaron.

The old man waved as he headed down the trail to the barn, and Maggie turned to Aaron as they climbed out of Daniel's truck.

"You need to run on and help Skinny with the feeding. This is the second day he's done it for you. And be sure and thank him."

Aaron shot a look of disappointment toward Daniel, who was busy unloading Maggie's bags from the bed of the truck.

"Aw, Mom, I want to stay with Daniel," he argued.

At the sound of his name Daniel glanced up. "Aaron, I'll be here for a few more minutes. You need to do what your mother tells you. Remember that little talk we had about making her happy?"

Aaron's petulant expression quickly faded. "Oh, yeah. You're right, Daniel. I'll be right back. Don't run off without telling me bye."

The boy raced away, and Maggie stared thoughtfully after him before she stepped over to Daniel. "What was that all about? What little talk? One of your telephone conversations?"

A faint smile creased Daniel's face. "No. That night after he went missing, I reminded him of how upset and worried he'd made you. And that he needed to make it up to you by obeying."

Maggie ran a shrewd gaze over his face. "Where did you learn about dealing with kids? You didn't have siblings."

He shrugged and grinned. "No. But I remember what it was like to be a mischievous little boy."

"You? Mischievous?" she teased. "I don't believe it."

He chuckled and reached for two more bags. As Maggie watched him lower them to the ground, she wanted to tell him what a good father he would make. But the words would sound suggestive to him, especially after last night. And she figured the best thing she could do now was try to keep things as light as possible between them.

Once he had all their bags on the ground, he refused to allow Maggie to carry even one of them into the house. So while he finished the chore, she went to the kitchen and made them each a glass of iced tea.

When she heard the front door open again, she called to him. "In here, Daniel."

Moments later he entered the kitchen and she held up the iced tea for him to see. "I thought you might like to drink something before you went home," she offered.

With a grateful smile, he walked over to where she was standing by the cabinets and took one of the glasses from her.

"Thanks, Maggie."

Funny how two little words were all he had to say to make her heart leap with pleasure. Dear heaven, she never dreamed she could ever feel this giddy or womanly. It was a powerful notion to know that this strong, sexy deputy wanted her in his bed. Especially when she was so much older than him.

"You're welcome," she murmured. "But I should be thanking you for giving Aaron such a wonderful weekend. I'm sure he'll never forget it."

His gaze met hers, then wandered downward to her lips. "Neither will I."

Suddenly Maggie was remembering, too. Remembering the intimate places his fingers and lips had touched her. And how the driving rhythm of his body had sent hers splintering into a million glittering diamonds.

Her heart thumping heavily, she said, "Daniel, I—"

She didn't finish as he stepped forward and slipped his fingers into her hair. She closed her eyes and sighed as he bent his head and kissed the side of her neck.

"When am I going to see you again?" he murmured next to her ear.

"I don't know." Her throat tightened with unbearable need and the logic that she couldn't always have what she wanted or needed.

"You—don't regret what happened, do you?" he murmured.

She tilted her head up, and their gazes locked.

"No. I don't regret even one moment. But I'm not sure it should happen again."

His fingers stroked her hair. His expression turned solemn. "I'm not so sure it should happen, either. But I don't think we'll be able to stop it. Do you?"

She turned her back to him, and he placed his glass on the counter, then put his hands on her shoulders.

"You make it sound like we have some sort of affliction we can't cure," she said with a bit of dismay.

"If I sound like that, I don't mean to. Just tell me—when will you see me again?"

She turned to face him, and the moment her eyes met his, she felt a sinking feeling of surrender. How did she ever expect to get over him when just looking at his face gave her such pleasure? How could she deny them time together, when all she wanted to do was wrap her arms around him and hold him forever?

Drawing in a shaky breath, she said, "I don't know. Call me tomorrow or the next day and we'll figure something out."

He bent his head and was kissing her softly when the sound of footsteps tapping across the back porch broke the silence.

Knowing Aaron was about to burst into the kitchen, the two adults pulled back and put a measure of distance between them.

The moment Aaron stuck his head around the door, he spotted Daniel and his mother standing near the kitchen sink. He raced over to them as he sucked in rapid breaths of air.

"Daniel, you're still here," Aaron said with relief. "I ran all the way from the barn! I thought you'd be gone."

Daniel had never had a connection to a child before and it still amazed him that Aaron seemed to consider him his hero or, at the very least, his mentor. The idea never failed to swell Daniel's chest.

He reached down and curled his thumb and forefinger around Aaron's chin. "I promised you I wouldn't leave. Remember what I told you about a man keeping his word?"

Aaron shot a furtive glance toward his mother before he turned his attention back to Daniel. "Yes sir, I remember."

Daniel released his hold on Aaron's chin and patted the boy's head. "Good. Now, it's time I was heading home. But I want to know one thing," he told the boy. "Did you have a good time this weekend?"

Aaron's eyes sparkled and he grinned. "Boy, did I ever! Thank you, Daniel! Thank you!"

Before Daniel guessed the child's intentions, Aaron's little arms were wrapped around his waist and he was holding on tightly.

For a moment the boy's unexpected display of affection caused a lump to form in Daniel's throat. He tried his best to swallow it down as he hugged Aaron's slender shoulders.

"Okay. I'm convinced that you liked the camping trip," Daniel said as he pried the boy's arms from around him. "And you're very welcome. I enjoyed it, too."

Aaron jumped back and bounced eagerly. "Does that mean we can go again soon?"

Daniel cast Maggie a covert glance. If he could spend every weekend in a tent with her, he'd be glad to drive for miles and build a camp. Hell, he'd stand on his head and sing just to get to kiss her again.

"Uh, maybe," he told Aaron. "We've got to rest up over this one first. And that means that I've got to say goodbye and drive home."

Aaron appeared to be faintly disappointed, but in a matter of seconds his expression brightened. "Okay. I'll walk out to the truck with you and we can say goodbye man-to-man-like."

Smiling, Daniel took him by the shoulder and

headed them toward the kitchen door. "Sounds good to me." He glanced back over his shoulder at Maggie. She was watching the two of them with an expression so wistful it nearly broke his heart. "Goodbye, Maggie."

"Goodbye, Daniel."

Besides being a big, tall man with a huge presence, Sheriff Perez was one of the most observant people whom Daniel had ever met in his entire life. It was no wonder that, on the following Monday morning, he took Daniel aside from his group of deputies.

"Come on into my office," he told Daniel after their regular Monday-morning meeting had broken up and officers were heading out of the building to follow the sheriff's orders.

"What have I done wrong now?" Daniel asked as he followed Quito Perez into the dimly lit room the sheriff called an office. It contained an old metal teacher's desk, a rolling chair that had seen better days and two wooden straight-back chairs with padded seats for visitors. One thing the people of San Juan County could say of Sheriff Perez, he believed in putting the taxpayers' dollars into fighting crime rather than decorating his office.

"You haven't done a thing wrong." The sheriff pointed to one of the visitor's chairs as he lowered his big frame into his own seat. "I just happened to notice you were very quiet this morning. I got the feeling that something is wrong. Want to tell me about it?"

Not really, Daniel thought. He didn't want to talk to anyone about Maggie. What he felt for her was too private, too special to put into words to a friend.

"There's nothing wrong. I just had a...long weekend. I'm not quite rested up yet."

The sheriff looked surprised. "Oh. Working cattle?"

Daniel owned only twenty head of cattle. He dabbled in raising them just for a hobby, and he'd already done all the vaccinating and dehorning he needed to do for this summer. Daniel focused his gaze on the toe of his black boot. "No."

The sheriff's brows lifted faintly. "Hell's afire, Daniel, don't tell me you broke the mold and went out partying."

Daniel's lips twisted as he prayed for some emergency to come in on 911. He felt like a kid in the principal's office. Not that he didn't like Quito Perez. He liked him very much. In fact, he'd admired the man for years and so had the people of San Juan County. That's why he'd been voted into office for his fifth term without any opposition to speak of. Still, that didn't mean he wanted to use the man as his personal therapist.

"No. Nothing like that. I took a little boy camping. Jess's nephew, as a matter of fact."

More surprise swept across the sheriff's face. "Hmm. You're talking about Maggie Ketchum's son. That must have been an experience."

Quito Perez made a point of knowing everyone in the county. It was no shocker that he understood who Jess's nephew was.

"It was," Daniel admitted. "That's why I'm still a little tired," he lied.

Hell, he wasn't tired. He could probably jump ten barbwire fences on foot and then ride a horse twenty miles before he felt fatigued. Whatever Maggie had done to him still had his blood hopping with energy. Yet he was worried, and he supposed that worry was the thing Quito had picked up on.

The sheriff rose from his creaking chair and walked over to a plastic percolator that had once been ivory in color but was now stained brown from coffee running down the sides. The old appliance should have been thrown away years ago, but the sheriff liked his coffee perked, and no one had the nerve to tell him he was old-fashioned.

As he poured the dark liquid into a mug he said, "Guess you talked with Maggie. How's she doing?"

Talked? For a second Daniel closed his eyes as erotic images of her nude body flashed through his mind. "Uh, fine. Actually, she went on the camping trip, too." Hell, there wasn't any use trying to hide anything from this man, Daniel decided crossly. He'd find it out, anyway. "I didn't feel comfortable taking Aaron by myself."

Quito slowly stirred cream into his coffee. "Hmm. That's nice. That's good."

Daniel rose from the visitor's chair and wiped his

hands down the front of his jeans. "I'd better go, Sheriff. The men have already left. And I'm supposed to be gathering evidence for that pawnshop robbery."

Turning, Quito motioned Daniel back into the chair. "Sit. The evidence will be there when you get there."

"But—"

"But nothing," he butted in brusquely. "If a beautiful woman like Maggie Ketchum went camping with you, then why do you look like you do?"

Daniel's thumb and forefinger thoughtfully stroked his jaw. "I didn't know I looked different."

The sheriff shook his head in a helpless way. "Well, this morning, when you were supposed to be listening to me, you were frowning and staring off into space. And now I see that the frown is still on your face. Why? What's that all about?"

"Oh hell, Sheriff, you don't want to hear any of this," Daniel muttered while he sent up another prayer for an emergency call. Even if it were only a cat up a tree, he would jump at the chance to race to the rescue.

Quito settled back in his chair. "Actually, I would. In fact, Jess has asked me many times what the deal is about you and women. Maybe it's time we both found out."

"Me and women," Daniel repeated irritably. "There is nothing."

"That's just it! Nothing!" The other man leaned

up in his chair. "A guy your age...who looks like you. It isn't normal for you to avoid women."

Daniel's frown grew deeper. "Well, I never tried to pretend I was anything close to normal."

The sheriff rose from his chair and walked behind Daniel in order to shut the door of the office. With their privacy assured, Quito rested his hand on Daniel's shoulder and shook it once with affection.

"Look, Daniel, this is man-to-man now. Not boss and employee. If you're upset for some reason over Maggie Ketchum, then maybe—"

"I'm not upset," Daniel interrupted, then groaned with misgivings. "Well, I suppose that's not entirely true. I'm worried. And I don't know what to do next. Sheriff, how do you make a woman understand how much you...love her?"

Quito gave Daniel's shoulder another pat, then walked back around the metal desk and took a seat. There were no family pictures on his desk or walls. No wife or children for him to go home to. In that way he was much like Daniel, only a few years older.

"If I knew that—" he paused and shook his head "—well, let's just say I wouldn't be sitting here alone."

By the time Wednesday came around, Maggie hadn't heard a word from Daniel, and she was beginning to wonder if she'd made a mistake about the deputy. Maybe he didn't want her that much after all, she couldn't help thinking. Maybe that night at the lake was more than enough sex for the soft-spoken Ute.

The notion had barely had time to thread through her brain when the phone next to her right elbow rang. Since she was at Victoria's clinic, doing her usual volunteering stint at bookkeeping, she certainly wasn't expecting to hear Daniel's voice on the line. And when she finally realized it was him, everything inside her felt as if it stopped. As she waited for him to speak, her heartbeat, her breathing, her voice quivered as though they were gripped by a strange force.

"You're a hard lady to keep up with," he said. "I called your home and the hospital. Finally a woman took pity on me and told me to try here. I didn't realize you worked for Victoria."

Finishing a convulsive swallow, she said, "It's not work. I volunteer every week to help her with the bookkeeping. Doctors have so much of it, you know."

"Yeah. Probably as much as deputies do."

She chuckled nervously. "Yeah. I thought...you'd decided not to call me. It's been three days since you left the house," she said.

She didn't sound accusing but, rather, fatalistic, and Daniel realized she couldn't be expecting much from him or even herself.

"I'm sorry, honey. I've been very busy and the time has gotten away from me. Did you miss me?"

Every hour, every second Maggie thought. Aloud she said, "Of course I did. I didn't like having to do my own cooking."

He chuckled. "Then maybe I can do something about that. Why don't you come over to my place for dinner? I have steaks in the refrigerator and brown beans in the slow cooker. I might even stir up some cornbread if you talk nice to me."

She couldn't stop the corners of her mouth from turning upward. These past three days she'd listened for the phone to ring. She wondered and waited and missed him terribly. It was joyous to hear his voice again and to know that he hadn't dismissed her from his life.

"Sounds like a real cowboy meal."

"Yeah, from a real Indian."

Since he wasn't a big teaser, his words put an even bigger smile on her face. "It sounds very nice, Daniel. But I have Aaron to deal with."

"Surely you've left him with a sitter before, or a relative. He's not a baby, Maggie."

The word *baby* pushed her thoughts to other things, and she rubbed her hand back and forth across her lower abdomen. Dear God, could she be pregnant now, she wondered.

"I know, Daniel. It's just that...he's so very fond of you. And if I tell him I'm going to see you, I'm sure he's going to have a fit to come with me."

He let out a heavy sigh. "Well, I wouldn't mind Aaron coming. I'm very fond of him, too. But I wanted this evening for the two of us, alone. I...there's something I want to talk to you about."

Gripping the phone, she straightened in her seat. "About what? Is something wrong?"

"Maggie, Maggie." His voice had lowered and

she decided he must have phoned from the sheriff's office. "Nothing is wrong. I don't want to go into it over the telephone. Can you be at my place by six?"

She had no idea what she was going to tell Aaron. She'd never been a dating mother and this was all very new for her and her son. But maybe Aaron would understand.

"All right. I'll be there," she said.

"Great. I'll see you then."

As Maggie put the phone receiver back on its hook, she looked up to see Victoria standing in front of the desk. Her brows were raised in a fashion that told Maggie the other woman must have heard at least a part of the conversation.

"Going out somewhere?"

Maggie smiled politely and looked down at the papers she'd been working on before Daniel's call. "Aren't you being a little too nosy?"

Victoria chuckled. "No. You're my sister-in-law. I have a right to be nosy about you. Are you going out with Daniel again?"

Maggie's head jerked upward. "Again! What do you mean again! I haven't been on a date with the man."

Victoria rolled her eyes. "Oh, you're right, it wasn't a date. It was a whole weekend."

Maggie closed her eyes and breathed deeply. "Please don't start."

"You are going out with him. That's why you were smiling when I stepped into the room."

Shuffling several papers together, Maggie stuffed

them into a manila folder and carried the lot over to a tall filing cabinet.

"Okay, I confess. The man is going to cook dinner for me."

Victoria gleefully rubbed her palms together, then suddenly stopped and frowned. "That's good. But what are you going to do with Aaron?"

"Good question. Got any ideas?"

The beautiful, dark-headed doctor contemplated Maggie's question for only a second. "As a matter of fact, I do. You can bring him by the ranch. Katrina adores playing with Aaron, and she can show him the new puppies that Sadie had last week. They're just now starting to open their eyes."

Maggie looked hopeful. "Oh, Aaron would love that. But are you sure, Victoria? You have so much to do already, and I know you count your time with Jess special."

Victoria's laughter trilled around the small space Maggie used for an office. "I do count it special. But with two small children, time with each other is hard to find. We have to wait until the lights go out, if you know what I mean. And even then we're not sure if Katrina will come toddling into the bedroom wanting to sleep with her parents. Dear heaven, by the time Sam starts walking we'll need a king-size mattress," she joked. "Believe me, one more child around the house isn't going to bother us. In fact, let him stay overnight and I'll drop him off at the T Bar K tomorrow. I need an excuse to visit Ross and Bella anyway."

"Thank you, Victoria. You're an angel."

Victoria laughed as she started out the door. "Don't let this white coat fool you," she said over her shoulder.

As her sister-in-law exited the room, Maggie very nearly collided with Nevada, who'd come in search of the doctor.

"Hey, doesn't anyone around here besides me do any work?" Nevada tossed the question at the two women.

Victoria paused in the open doorway long enough to motion her head toward Maggie. "We do. But we were just discussing a date." She turned a pointed look on her young nurse. "Have you given Mr. Logan his injection?"

Nevada nodded. "He's waiting for you in Room 1," she informed her boss, then looked back and forth between Victoria and Maggie. "And what kind of date are you talking about? With a man?"

Victoria laughed. "Is there any other kind?"

Maggie groaned as Victoria walked away and Nevada entered the tiny office. Not again, she thought.

The young Hispanic nurse, with flashing brown eyes and waist-length hair coiled atop her head, jammed her hands on her curvy hip as she looked slyly at Maggie. "Are we talking about a date with Mr. Cool?"

Maggie's nostrils flared. If the truth were known Nevada would be a much better match for Daniel. She was much younger and full of spirit. Her face and hair were beautiful and her figure was hourglass and then some. The nurse didn't want to be tied down. And from all that she'd gathered, neither did Daniel. So why was he bothering with Maggie Ketchum, she wondered.

"If you mean Daniel Redwing. That's right."

She made a tsking noise with her tongue. "Oh, Lord, Lord, if I were only in your shoes. I'd be walking on air."

Maggie was walking on air, but her state of mind was a result of somersaulting nerves. She could only think of Daniel as forbidden fruit, and she couldn't begin to guess what was going to happen to her now that she'd had a taste of him.

"It would probably be better if you were in my shoes," Maggie told her. "I really don't have any business going on a date. Especially with a man like Daniel." She didn't have any business making love to him, either, she thought. But she had and, as she'd told Daniel, she wasn't going to regret that now.

Nevada frowned with disbelief. "Why do you say that?"

Maggie sighed. "Because I'm too old for him. And I have...well, past issues."

Shaking her head vehemently, Nevada stepped over to the desk and covered Maggie's hand with her smooth brown one.

"You are far from being too old, dear friend. And the past is just that—the past. Maybe it's time for you to leave that all behind you and start fresh, hmm?"

Like the Utes' Bear Dance, Maggie thought.

Leave a feather on a tree and along with it all the fears and troubles of the years before. How wonderful that would be, if only it could truly happen and she could forget the devastation of losing the man she'd loved.

Chapter Ten

Maggie arrived at Daniel's five minutes early and parked her vehicle in front of the old, hacienda-style ranch house. The front of the structure was shaded with a straight row of poplars while at one end an array of choya, yucca, prickly pear and stovepipe cacti grew wide and tall against the outer wall. The porch was also dotted with pots of succulents growing in the evening sun.

A black-and-white dog that appeared to be some sort of collie was lying next to the front door. Maggie presumed the animal was friendly and reached down to pat its head before she rang the doorbell.

Daniel promptly opened the door, and she found herself greeting him with a nervous little laugh.

"Hello, Daniel. I know I'm early. But the drive didn't take me as long as I anticipated."

"I'm glad," he said simply, and pushed the screen door wide for her to enter.

The house was deliciously cool and dim enough to make Maggie nearly blinded after the bright sunlight outside. She blinked and looked around her as images began to appear. Ancient wooden shutters were closed against the western windows to block out the heat, and the low roof was made up of dark wooden beams.

"This is so lovely," Maggie exclaimed as she turned slowly to survey the living room. "How old is this house, anyway?"

"I'm not sure. I've tried to find out the exact age. But no one can find accurate records. I'm guessing at least 120 years old. The story goes that a south Texas rancher moved up here and built the place to escape the heat of the Lone Star State. Trouble was he brought a herd of Brahmans and none of them survived the cold."

"How sad," Maggie replied. "Did he have a wife and children?"

Daniel slipped his hand against her upper back and guided her in the direction of the kitchen. "Yes, I think so. Because it was a son of his that eventually sold this place to Norman Prescott, an Aztec native. Norman's in the nursing home now, but he still remembers the family."

The two of them turned into a wide, short hallway

with arched openings leading off in several directions. He nudged her to take the one to the right, and soon they were standing in an elongated room built along the back of the house. Where the cabinets ended, a row of several low windows began, and Maggie was instantly enamored with the view of the mountains beyond the small glass panes.

"How beautiful," she murmured and hurried over to a round pine table situated near the windows. "How do you get anything done, Daniel? I'd be sitting here all day, looking and daydreaming."

He came up behind her and slid his arms around her waist. "I do sit here and daydream at breakfast." He lifted a hand and pointed. "See that tall peak over to the right. Your home sits down in the crease below it. I look at that spot and think of you."

Twisting around in his arms, she slid her arms up around his neck. "Daniel, I've never had a man say the sweet things to me that you do."

A sexy chuckle rumbled up from his chest. "Don't get me confused, Maggie. There's nothing sweet about me."

"Maybe I should be the judge of that," she said as she rose on tiptoe and kissed his lips.

His hands gathered at the back of her waist and for long moments he held her close answering the seductive search of her mouth.

When the kiss finally ended, he looked down at her. "My, my that was quite a greeting," he said with a smile. "Want to try it again?"

Laughing softly, she pushed out of his embrace. "No. We might never have any supper. And I'm very hungry."

She walked over to the gas range where a large iron skillet was heating over a blue flame. Two thick and seasoned rib eyes were sitting on the cabinet counter, waiting to be cooked.

"I was waiting for you to arrive so the steak would be hot. How do you like yours cooked?" he asked.

She stood to one side as he joined her at the range. "A little rare."

"Good. So do I. This won't take long."

He tossed the cuts of beef into the skillet, and the meat instantly seared. The scent wafted upward, and Maggie's stomach growled with anticipation.

"Tell me where you keep your dishes and I'll set the table for us," she told him.

He glanced over at her. "No need. It's already done. In the dining room. I wanted to impress you," he added.

Just standing here next to him impressed her, Maggie thought. He was neither a cocky or wordy person, yet he had a physical presence that always bowled her over. Just as it was overwhelming her at this very moment.

Tonight he was dressed casually in a pair of Levi's and a navy-blue T-shirt. The muscles of his chest and arms had the thin fabric stretched taut against him and she could hardly keep her eyes or her hands off him.

A few minutes later the steaks were cooked, and the two of them went to the dining room to eat their meal. Like the kitchen, the dining room had several windows near the table and chairs. Only this view was of red buttes and a wide, empty mesa filled with nothing but cacti and sagebrush. The picture in front of them was rough and lonely but mesmerizing.

Maggie said, "That Texan must have liked the scenery here. He had plenty of windows built in the house."

Daniel nodded as he filled her plate with pinto beans. "Guess he didn't realize that harshness oftentimes accompanies beauty."

Her expression thoughtful, she glanced at him. "How did you wind up with this place? Does it have much acreage?"

"About two thousand acres. Not really enough to graze much livestock. I have a couple of horses and twenty cows running on it now. And that's too many. But I grain feed often."

She nodded and he went on. "As for the house, around about the time Norman turned seventy he had a stroke and couldn't take care of the place. His relatives advised him to sell the place, but he couldn't give it up. Not right then. He sold off several thousand acres, leaving the two thousand and the house and barns. When he finally went into the nursing home, I asked him about leasing the place. He agreed and for five years I leased. But then one day I went to visit him, and he offered to sell the whole thing to me. Even offered to let the rent that I'd paid those five years to go in on the price. I couldn't turn that kind of deal down."

Maggie swallowed a bite of her steak before she answered, "This man must be very generous."

Daniel nodded. "And one of the very best friends I've ever had. Maybe you'd like to go with me to visit him sometime," he suggested, then immediately frowned. "Or maybe you wouldn't. Not too many people will go into nursing homes."

Reaching across the table, she squeezed his hand. "Don't be silly. I volunteer at the hospital every week. I know what it's like to see sick people and old people in need. I like to think I can help them in some way. Even if it's just handing them a newspaper."

His brown eyes softened with admiration as they swept over her face. "I'm so glad you came tonight. I've missed you, Maggie. I wanted to call before, but the department has been overloaded with work. I'm surprised I got this evening off."

"I'm glad you did," she said softly.

He sliced into his own steak and smeared it into a dollop of steak sauce. "What about Aaron? Where is he tonight?"

"At Jess and Victoria's. She offered to babysit. They have new puppies. Aaron was excited about that."

"He didn't give you a bad time about wanting to come, too?"

Maggie shook her head and then blushed. "Not at

all. He has this idea that we are now boyfriend and girlfriend and we need to be alone."

"Well, we are...boyfriend and girlfriend, aren't we?"

She sighed. "Daniel, I've been thinking and—"

He shot her a pointed look and she stopped in the middle of her sentence. "I've been thinking, too," he said. "But let's not talk about all that now. Let's finish our supper."

Maggie was more than happy to oblige. If he asked her to have an affair with him here at the supper table, her appetite for food would fly right out the window.

"All right, Daniel. We'll talk later."

Nearly an hour later, after several cups of coffee and dessert that Daniel had purchased at the bakery in Aztec, Daniel invited her outside to view the small courtyard at the back of the house.

Maggie was instantly charmed and surprised when she saw a square redbrick patio around a small trickling fountain fashioned in the form of a nude angel holding up a basket of fruit. Apparently the fountain and the patio had been there for years. Arid plants and grasses, some of which were blooming, grew thick and tall, almost hiding the divine figure.

Lawn furniture made of bent willow branches sat in a grouping not far from the trickling sound of the water. Daniel gestured for her to take a seat in one.

"You have surprised me over and over tonight," she said as she sank onto the padded cushion. "I never expected you to have such a...home."

"What did you expect? Strobe lights and mirrors? Or a tepee with a buffalo hide for the door?"

For a moment she thought she'd offended him and that he was angry with her. But then she caught the glimpse of his white teeth as he smiled in the darkness and she realized he was teasing her.

"Well, neither actually. I just expected your place to be—well, like a man who is rarely here, who wouldn't bother to have lawn chairs because he doesn't socialize or have the time to, even if he did."

He didn't sit in the accompanying chair to hers. Instead, he meandered over to a clump of purple sage and plucked off a bloom.

"I am a busy man," he conceded. "But I do have friends over from time to time. Jess and Victoria come to see me. And my grandfather on occasions. Sometimes I get Norman out of the nursing home and bring him out here, just so he can see what the old place still looks like."

"What does your grandfather think of this place?" she asked curiously.

Daniel shrugged. "He thinks its pretty grand. But still, he'd rather have me living on Ute land. I tell him this is Ute land. I own it."

"What about your mother?"

A soft night breeze was beginning to blow down from the north and cool the shadowed yard behind the hacienda. Daniel watched it tease Maggie's red hair and flutter the hem of her skirt against her legs.

She was a very beautiful woman. And each time he looked at her, he wondered where his boldness to have her had come from. She was far out of his league and it would probably make more sense if he told her tonight that they should make their relationship nothing more than friendship. Yet that was the last thing he intended to tell her, and it made him quake inside to imagine how she was going to react.

His moccasins made no sound on the red brick as he walked over to her chair and squatted on his heels in front of her.

Handing her the sage bloom, he said, "You deserve roses. But the sage is strong and can withstand any type of weather you throw at it. Like you, my lovely Maggie. You're a strong woman. You've just never realized it yet."

She took the pungent blooms and lifted them to her nose. The scent was wild and sweet and strong and Maggie wondered if that was the way he thought of her. The idea made her pulse beat with warm pleasure. "Is that what you wanted to tell me?" she asked.

Shaking his head, he planted his hands on both arms of the chair and leaned into her. Brushing his lips against hers, he murmured, "No. That's not it. We'll talk later. Right now I just want you."

His stark admission was as effective as the erotic touch of his lips, and she groaned with need, then whispered, "And I want you, Daniel Redwing."

In a rough but reverent way, his lips seized hers at the same time his hands slid into her hair. Cradling the back of her head, he feasted on the sweetness of her lips until her hands were pulling at his shoulders, urging him to come closer.

Finally he ended the kiss and, breathing heavily, he rose to his feet, then reached for her hand. Maggie slipped her fingers around his, and he gently tugged her to her feet and into his arms.

With his hands roaming her back, crushing her to him, Daniel kissed her again, until the ache in his loins vibrated through his whole body.

"Let's go over here," he whispered.

Taking her by the hand, he led her away from the tinkling fountain to a spot on the ground-level porch that ran the length of the house. A sturdy chaise lounge built of the same willow limbs and cushioned with weatherproof pads sat at an angle and was shaded by the deep shadow of the porch roof.

He nudged her down on the seat, then once again he squatted in front of her and began to undo the buttons on the gauzy white blouse she was wearing.

She gasped with surprise. "Daniel! What are you doing?"

A low chuckle rolled past his lips. "Undressing you."

Her eyes widened. "But we're outside! And it's not even dark yet."

In spite of her protest, he pushed the material down off her shoulders, then traced his fingers into the soft, deep valley between her breasts.

"The sun has set and the shadows are long. There's no one around here for miles. Except me and you."

"Oh."

Her sigh of relief whispered against the side of his neck as he bent forward and nuzzled his lips along her delicate collarbone.

"Then I guess it doesn't matter what we do, right here, outside, in the open," she said distractedly as the touch of his lips slid downward over her bare breast.

"Anything you want, my darling."

His words were muffled, but that didn't matter. Maggie had heard them, and the knowledge that he aimed to please her was like a potent drink burning the pit of her stomach.

Arching toward him, she buried her fingers in his thick black hair and urged him toward her breast. The sharp tug of his mouth sent shards of unbearable heat to the very core of her femininity. Crying out with pleasure, she tried to pull him closer, to gather his body against hers.

Pulling slightly away from her, Daniel quickly shed his clothes, then hurriedly undressed Maggie. She had never made love in the outdoors, and the feel of the evening air brushing against her skin was like a velvet cloak sliding over and around her.

When he joined her on the wide lounge, he clamped her naked body tightly against his and buried his lips in the curve of her shoulder.

"You taste like cream, Maggie. Sweet, thick cream. The kind that goes straight to your heart and causes all sorts of problems."

She hung on to him as his lips continued their foray over the mound of one breast and down the faint indention in the middle of her abdomen.

"I don't want to be a problem," she said, her voice languid with desire.

"If you call wanting you twenty-four hours, seven days a week a problem, then I've got it."

She watched his dark head descend her pale torso, and her heart began to thud at an even faster pace. Blood thrummed at her temples, in the tips of her fingers and deep in her loins.

"Daniel, don't keep making me wait," she said with an edgy gasp.

His hands slid to her inner thighs and nudged them apart. "Shh. Don't be so impatient my little night bird."

His fingers touched her, then as he stroked her, teased her until the desperate ache inside her became an unbearable throb, the tiny moan lodged in her throat grew until it burst past her lips in a low, needy groan.

Maggie writhed against his fingers for relief, but suddenly he took the pleasure away and she opened her eyes just in time to see his head burying itself between her thighs.

Shock parted her lips, but she didn't have a chance to protest. Not that she would or even could. The feel of his tongue sliding into the most intimate part of her was like a thousand orchestras crashing to a crescendo inside her head. And in only a matter of moments her whole body was splintering into tiny pieces of bliss.

"Oh. Oh, Daniel. Daniel," she finally murmured as the pieces of her body settled back together. "You're too good to me."

"I want to be better. Much better."

Easing over her, he brought his wet lips down to hers, and as he kissed her he joined their bodies with slow, exquisite pleasure and they made love until the sky was filled with stars and the mesa grew dark.

Once their bodies cooled and the sweat on their skin had dried, Daniel carried her into the house and placed her in the middle of his bed.

As he switched on a small shaded lamp at the head of the bed, Maggie looked curiously around her at the chinked wooden walls and the tile floors that had shifted to a slight tilt but still hadn't lost their luster.

The cover on the bed was a handwoven blanket similar to what she'd seen at the Hubbell Trading Post on the Navajo Reservation. The colors were gray and burgundy and yellow, and the faint nubby texture of the thread was perfect for the rustic old house.

"Where did you get the blanket? I've seen some like this, except smaller. The price tag on them was several thousand dollars," she said as she ran her hand over the blanket. "This one would cost a fortune."

He lay down next to her and propped his head on his hand. "My mother wove it. I'm sure it looks Navajo to you, but I won't tell her you thought so. She's a proud Ute, you see."

Smiling softly, she reached out and touched his cheek. "I like your house, Daniel. Especially the back porch," she added provocatively.

Scooting closer, he ran a hand over her bare hip, and his eyes glinted with remembered pleasure. "I'm glad you like it. Especially the porch."

Curling her arm around his waist, she rested her cheek next to his chest. "On the phone this afternoon, you mentioned that you wanted to talk to me about something. Was that a ploy to get me over here, or did you really have something to tell me?"

His hand moved from its resting place on her hip to slide up her spine. As he began to speak, his fingers kneaded the nape of her neck.

"It wasn't a ploy, Maggie. I'm not a man who has hidden agendas or tactics. I speak what I feel. Sometimes that gets me into deep trouble. But that's just the way I am."

Yes, he was a straightforward sort of man, Maggie thought. Never at any time would she think he was lying or being evasive with her.

"I believe you."

He rubbed his cheek against the crown of her head. "Good. Because I have been thinking long and hard about you and me. And I've come to a decision."

Her heart was literally knocking in her throat as

she tilted her head back and met his gaze. "Daniel, what do you mean? What sort of decision?"

Using his fingers, he combed the wayward hair from her brow, then bent his head ever so slightly and pressed a kiss to her forehead. "I don't want us to go on like this. I want us to be together. All the time."

Maggie's blue eyes softened, then misted over. "I think—I don't know if I want us to have this conversation, Daniel. The night has been so beautiful. Aaron is at Jess and Victoria's. I don't have to rush home to be with him. Please lets not ruin this time together with an argument."

A wry smile moved his lips. "How do you know there will be an argument?"

She grimaced. "Because. You're going to ask me to move in with you...to have an affair with you and I'm going to have to tell you no."

His face went smooth, and after a moment he rolled onto his back and joined his hands in the middle of his chest. Since he was only wearing a pair of white boxer shorts, his bronze body was exposed to Maggie's view. She drank in the gorgeous sight of him as he thoughtfully twiddled his thumbs.

"So. You think that's what I want," he said.

She heaved out a breath. "Well...yes. It is, isn't it?"

Her question seemed to snap him out of his casual pose and he rolled back toward her and took hold of the side of her waist.

"Maggie! You are not a woman who could have

an affair. Not with any man. I would never ask you to do such a thing. I would never want you to…to lower yourself."

Suddenly, as she looked into the depths of his brown eyes, she felt lost and confused. He was looking at her as though she were something precious, too precious to let go.

"I don't…understand. If that's not what you want, then what are you trying to tell me? That we need to end our relationship now? Tonight?"

His palm moved over her lips to prevent her from saying more, and she looked up at him in confusion.

With an impatient groan, he said, "Maggie, I'm trying to tell you that I love you. I want us to get married. I want us to have a family. Not just with Aaron. But for us to have more children…together."

Maggie was so stunned by his words that she went absolutely limp against the mattress. Daniel wanted to marry her? He wanted them to have babies? To share the future as man and wife?

After Hugh's death, she never, in her wildest dreams, imagined her life starting over. Never dreamed she would ever feel a man's hand touch her with love and desire, or consider the possibility of carrying his child inside her.

She had fallen in love with Daniel. There was no sense in even trying to deny that, to herself or to him. But being in love with a man wasn't the same as being his wife or making a family together. Those were risky objectives. She'd loved and lost. She'd found out firsthand how fleeting life really was. She couldn't go through that all over again.

"Maggie? Don't you have anything to say?"

Tears began to roll down her cheeks as she turned her gaze on Daniel's face. "I'm sorry, Daniel. I can't marry you. Now or ever."

Chapter Eleven

Daniel sat up in the middle of the bed and stared at her with such a wounded expression, Maggie's tears flowed even harder.

"Why?"

It was just like him, she thought, to expect one simple question to answer everything.

Wiping her cheeks with the back of her hand, she raised herself up to a sitting position while silently wishing for a robe. Being naked made her feel even more vulnerable to him.

"Because…I never plan to marry again. I made myself that promise a long time ago."

"Promises can be broken. Especially when they're made for the wrong reason."

Emotions jabbed at her and caused her gaze to drift downward to the woven blanket beneath them. "Daniel, you know what I went through with Hugh. Or at least I think you understand how that devastated me. How these past years have been like a deep, yawning canyon with no way to climb out."

His fingers came beneath her chin and tugged her gaze back around to his. His eyes were unblinking as he spoke. "What does that have to do with me? With us?"

She made a sound of frustration. "Don't you understand, Daniel? If we did get married and have children and then—" she paused and drew in a deep, painful breath "—and then I lost you for some reason…I…"

Maggie couldn't go on. She couldn't bear to think of losing this man in any way.

"You couldn't what?" Daniel pressed her.

Shaking her head, she whispered, "I couldn't go on, Daniel. I couldn't go on without you."

Her tears began to flow slowly and silently down her face. Daniel drew her into his arms and smoothed his hand over her rumpled hair. "Maggie, if you felt this way, why did you ever sleep with me?"

Clinging tightly to his shoulders, she pressed her cheek next to his. "Because you're a very persuasive man, Daniel. And because I love you."

As soon as she uttered the word, he went stock-still, and within his chest, she could feel the beat of his heart pounding like an ancient Ute war drum preparing for battle.

Tilting her head back, he looked into her eyes. "I love you, too, Maggie. So very much. Dear God, you think you're afraid? In my entire life I never expected to say those words to a woman. I have always prayed for the Great Spirit to guide me away from a woman like you." His lips twisted wryly. "I guess I didn't pray hard enough. Or He isn't listening."

"Why would you be afraid, Daniel? You've never been married. Never lost anyone."

His eyes suddenly hardened. "Only my father. And I saw how it was to grow up with just one parent, without a father to guide me, to teach me how to be a good man, a good husband, a good father. The only things he did teach me were about alcohol and slovenliness and abuse. And to pray not to be like him."

"Oh, Daniel," she whispered in a choked voice.

He stroked her cheek. "For all these years, I was afraid to get involved, to love any woman. I knew that Robert Redwing's blood ran through my veins and that I probably wasn't capable of having and caring for a family any more than he was. But then I met you, and I love you so much, Maggie, that I have to believe I can be those things."

Her heart was suddenly weeping with both joy and sadness. "Oh, my darling, you *are* all those things. I have no doubt about that. You'd be a wonderful husband and father. But—"

A rueful sound of agony slipped past her lips and

she buried her face against the side of his neck while her arms clung fiercely to his rib cage.

He traced the tiny bumps of her spine with his fingertips. "But what?"

She didn't answer immediately. Because she didn't know how to explain to him about the deep-seated fear she held inside her.

"I don't want to go through the pain of losing you, Daniel. It would hurt too much. Do you understand?"

With a hand at the back of her head, he urged her to look at him. His face was solemn, but there was a soft glow of love in his eyes that Maggie couldn't turn away from.

"I understand that I want you. And you want me." He brought his lips next to hers as he spoke again, this time in a low, husky voice, "Let's not talk anymore, my Maggie. I want to love you. I want to wake up in the morning and see your face on my pillow. Don't ruin that for me. For us."

She gave him the answer he wanted by tugging him down on the bed and placing her lips over his.

The next morning it was past sunrise when Maggie awoke in Daniel's bed. The sheet covering her nude body was mottled with light that was filtered by the thin curtain at the window. The scent of freshly made coffee filled the room.

The space next to her was empty, and she wondered how long he'd been out of bed. It was not good that she'd stayed overnight, she thought. But she had not been able to resist him last night. And she was so hungry to be loved by him that she hadn't wanted to give up the precious time of being in his arms.

Wistfully Maggie drew her fingers across the empty spot where he'd lain, and her heart jerked with regret. Daniel was going to take her staying as a sign of surrender. He was going to think she'd changed her mind about marrying him. But she couldn't change her mind. To marry him would be disastrous. She'd drive him crazy with her constant worrying. Every time he walked out the door, she'd drive herself crazy with fear that something was going to happen to him. It was unreasonable fear but, just the same, it was there inside her.

On the foot of the iron bedstead, Daniel had carefully draped her clothing. The thoughtful gesture touched her ragged emotions and stung her eyes with tears. She took a deep breath and was about to push back the sheet to get out of bed when Daniel entered the room.

Clutching the white sheet to her naked breasts, she leaned back against the pillow and waited for him to come stand beside the bed. He was wearing a pair of Levi's with no shirt or shoes. There was a steaming cup of coffee in his hand and a sexy grin on his face, and she was shocked to feel her own body stir with excitement at the sight of him.

"Good morning, Maggie. I thought you might like a cup of coffee."

She looked around as though the bedroom was the last place for drinking anything. "In bed?"

"It's the best place for coffee. And other things," he added slyly. Then, reaching for the pillow next to her, he motioned for her to lean up.

Maggie leaned forward and he punched the pillow up behind her back. She felt like a pampered queen as she took the hot coffee from him.

With one hand she pushed the tangled hair from her eyes while she carefully sipped at the dark, steaming brew. "You shouldn't be spoiling me like this, Daniel. A woman could get very used to this kind of treatment."

He sat down on the edge of the mattress near the crook of her waist. Goose bumps rushed over her skin as he reached over and ran the back of his forefinger up and down her bare arm.

"That's my intention."

Clasping the cup with both hands, she stared down at its contents instead of his face. "I hope you don't think—" She stopped and turned pleading eyes up at him. "I haven't changed my mind about marrying you, Daniel."

He studied her with a quiet gentleness that wrung a tear from her heart. "Because you're afraid."

She breathed deeply and nodded. "I'd drive you crazy with my fear, Daniel. I'd drive both of us crazy. And then you'd end up hating me. And I couldn't stand that." She looked at him with fresh hope. "Maybe we could—just keep things like this. Maybe just seeing each other occasionally would be better."

His expression was stone smooth. "Would that be enough for you?"

Her mind was suddenly jammed with images of Daniel kissing her, touching her breasts and entering her body with a reverent hunger that took her breath away. No, if she spent every hour of every day with him it wouldn't be enough.

"Not really," she murmured with regret.

He reached up and pushed his long brown fingers into her hair. "It wouldn't be enough for me, either. This morning when I woke and you were lying next to me, I looked at you and knew that this was how it had to always be."

The love she heard in his words only squeezed her heart with pain. Blinking at her stinging eyes, she leaned over and placed the half-empty coffee cup on the nightstand.

"It can't be like that, Daniel."

His lips spread to a thin line. "Why? Because I'm Ute and you're a Ketchum?" he asked bitterly.

Maggie gasped as she turned back to him. "That's...a despicable thing to say to me! Especially with me sitting here naked in your bed!"

His expression softened. "Having sex with me isn't the same as marrying me. Think about it, Maggie."

So he believed she was just using him to satisfy her own physical needs? The idea floored her.

But that's the way it looks to him. You were willing to spend the night making love to him, but you're not willing to take his name.

The inner voice barking back at her made her stop and take a second breath.

"You being Ute has nothing to do with it. I'm terrified and you know it!"

She climbed out of bed and jerked her panties off the foot rail. As Daniel watched her step into them, he said, "What are you afraid of exactly? That I'll be like Robert Redwing? That I'll turn into a sot and leave you and Aaron behind?"

Maggie glared at him. "No. Nothing like that. I'm terrified of seeing you put six feet underground. Of knowing that I'd never see you, hear you, touch you ever again!"

Rising from the bed, he held up his hands in a helpless gesture. "Why would you worry about that? I'm very healthy and reasonably young. Are you preoccupied with death?"

Was she? It was hard not to be when every day she looked around her and saw what one fatal moment had done to her life. "I don't know. It's touched my life in a horrible way, Daniel. First my father and then Hugh. Tucker and Amelia are gone now, too. And even poor Noah's life ended on the T Bar K. Sometimes…sometimes I'm afraid it's not meant for me to…to have a family—any family."

His expression was pained as he went to her. "I'm not Hugh, Maggie."

"No. You're young and vibrant. But accidents can happen and you're a big target with that badge you wear on your chest." Shaking her head, she rubbed a hand across her burning eyes. “Besides,” she muttered, “I’m too old for you.”

“That’s stupid.”

“Look at my breasts,” she ordered.

“I am. They’re beautiful.” He cupped his hand around one rounded globe.

She groaned. “Maybe in your eyes. But they’re not young and perky. I’m not even sure if I can get pregnant now. And you want children.”

His hand slid protectively to her lower belly. “You’re probably pregnant with our child right now. We haven’t used birth control,” he reminded her.

Maggie stifled a groan. Last night she’d been so eager to make love to him, she’d forgotten all about using any sort of protection. The man was changing her, and after these past several years of dull regularity the idea scared her.

“Maybe that’s for the best. Maybe you’ll see that I can’t get pregnant and you’ll forget about me.”

She fastened her bra and adjusted the straps on her shoulders. She could feel him watching her quietly and thoughtfully as she stepped into her short skirt and buttoned the matching blouse over it.

“That would not make me forget you. Nothing could. And if you are not fertile, we’ll adopt.”

Amazed at his generosity, she looked at him. “You have an answer for everything, don’t you?”

He stepped closer and pulled her into his arms. “Everything except how to make you say yes,” he whispered.

Maggie was certain her whole body was going to break apart with pain and she turned her back to him before he could see the tears in her eyes. "I have to be home to meet Aaron when Victoria drops him off."

He released his hold on her upper arms, and she fled the bedroom and raced outside to her car. As she drove away, she expected to feel some measure of relief, some sense that once she got back home, her life would return to normal. But those were foolish expectations. Now that she'd fallen in love with Daniel Redwing nothing would ever be the same.

The San Juan County Sheriff's Department was housed in a redbrick building just off Main Street in Aztec. Behind the offices was a section of jail cells and behind those a huge parking area where most all the county lawmen parked their personal vehicles.

Two mornings after Maggie had left Daniel's house, he pulled into the parking area and killed the engine to his truck. The weather was cloudy and cool for early June, and he'd driven into work with the window down. He was about to roll it up and climb out of the vehicle when Jess Hastings, the undersheriff, approached him.

"You look like hell this morning, Redwing. What's the matter?"

Daniel glared at his boss and good friend. "Thanks for the nice greeting. That's just what I needed to start the day."

Jess chuckled as Daniel slid to the ground and slammed the vehicle door shut.

"Do you want me to lie to you?"

The two men turned and started toward the building. As they walked Daniel glanced over at him. "I want you to keep your observations to yourself."

Jess saluted from the brim of his cream-colored Stetson. "Yes, sir. Gotcha."

Daniel rolled his eyes, and Jess slapped him affectionately on the shoulder. "What *is* the matter with you, Daniel? Didn't get any sleep?"

"A little. I'm just tired, that's all. That damn pawnshop robbery has caused me several stacks of paperwork. I have a feeling some of the items old Lucias reported missing might be fictitious."

The two men reached the back entrance of the building, and Jess pushed a glass door open, motioning for Daniel to precede him into a narrow hallway.

"Come on down to my office and drink some coffee," Jess suggested. "Quito isn't going to be here for another thirty minutes."

At first Daniel started to decline the invitation. He didn't want Jess questioning him about Maggie, who just happened to be his sister-in-law. But other than Quito, Jess was his very best friend and had been for many years. He couldn't shun him just because he felt like a dead man.

"What's the matter with Quito? He's usually here at the crack of dawn," Daniel said. "I don't know of anyone more dedicated to his job."

Jess looked over at the small table holding the coffeepot. The glass carafe was full and there was a small box of pastries sitting next to it. The secretaries made sure the two sheriffs and the chief deputy were well taken care of.

"Oh, good," Jess commented. "Rita has already made coffee. Let's eat."

Daniel dragged up a metal chair and plopped his lanky body into it while Jess poured the coffee.

"I don't want anything. I've already had breakfast." Which had only been more coffee, but Daniel wasn't going to tell Jess that. The other man would be trying his best to stuff him with bear claws. And the way Daniel felt this morning the pastries would probably claw their way up again.

"So have I, but that doesn't mean I can't eat again," Jess remarked.

Daniel shook his head and accepted the cup of black coffee his friend held out to him.

"What are you up to today?" Daniel asked him.

Jess lowered himself into the seat behind a wooden desk. It was scattered with papers, cups, pencils and pens, manuals and reports. Daniel had never seen the man's desk cleaned and everything put in order. But he always got the job done. Always.

"I think I'm going to have to go with Quito to Farmington. They've got someone in jail who we have under warrant, but they don't want to give him up. I think Quito wants to do a little arguing with the judge." He sipped his coffee, then settled his gaze on Daniel's tired face. "What about yourself? How is it going with the pawnshop robbery?"

"I'm going to have a little talk with the prime suspect this morning."

"Who?"

"James Renaldo. You know. He has that tire shop across from Lucias's building."

Jess nodded grimly. "Yeah, he's a shady character. I've always believed he runs a chop shop in there at night, but we've never been able to catch him. You better be careful, Daniel. If the guy thinks you're on to him, he might just hole up in there with a gun."

"I'll be careful," Daniel promised.

"Hmm, well, the way you look, you're too tired to dodge a bullet."

Daniel didn't say anything to that, and Jess ate half a jelly doughnut before he said, "Aaron stayed the night with us the other night. Katrina had a blast. I think she wore the poor boy out. She likes to wrestle and she's not above pulling hair."

Daniel simply nodded and Jess went on, "Aaron told us all about your camping trip. It was obvious he had a great time. You should feel proud of yourself, Daniel. Aaron, well, he's missed out on so much without having his father around. And we can tell he thinks the world of you."

Daniel stared into his cup. "And I think the world of him."

"What about his mother?"

Daniel hadn't been expecting such a frank question, and his head jerked straight up. "You really expect me to answer that?"

Jess polished off the doughnut, then went back over to the coffee table and fished another one from the box. "Daniel, do you remember back when Noah Rider's remains were first found on the T Bar K? I had a murder investigation on my mind and all you could do was urge me to make things right with Victoria. I'm getting the feeling that it's your turn for a little personal badgering."

Daniel remembered the time well. The whole county had been in an uproar thinking a murderer was on the loose. So much had happened since then. Victoria and Jess marrying and having a son. Ross and Bella getting married. And then Seth and Corrina. Seemed everyone that he cared anything about had gotten a family of their own. Except him.

Releasing a long breath, Daniel said, "There's no sense in me trying to deny anything to you, Jess. I'm in love with Maggie. I asked her to marry me. But she refused, and now—well, I called her last night and she says she thinks it would be better if we didn't see each other at all! Damn it, Jess, why is the woman so stubborn?"

Wry sympathy colored Jess's faint smile. "You just said the word, Daniel. *Woman.* That explains everything. You never know how they're going to react about things. But don't worry about it. Maggie's been through hell—just give her a little time. She'll come around to loving you."

Daniel got up from his chair and walked over to the dusty window looking out over the parking area.

As he stared absently at the vehicles, he said, "She already says she loves me."

Jess frowned. "Then what the hell is holding her back?"

Daniel pinched the bridge of his nose. He'd never felt so drained or defeated in his life. He knew he had to snap out of it or his work would suffer. It would be unforgivable if he let someone in the department down just because he wasn't thinking straight.

"Fear. Plain and simple."

"Oh. Well—"

Before Jess could finish his remark, footsteps were suddenly pounding down the hallway and another deputy stuck his head in Jess's office and shouted, "The sheriff has been shot! Two miles south of town on 544!"

Neither Jess nor Daniel bothered to question the deputy. They both raced out the back entrance of the building and jumped into the closest squad car they could find.

As Jess stomped on the gas, Daniel got on the radio to see what he could find out from the dispatcher. *Two shots fired. Sheriff is down. Ambulance is on the way. Suspect got away.*

"What the hell has happened?" Daniel threw the question at Jess as the other man flipped on the siren and sped through the first red traffic light.

"We'll find out in a minute. Let's just pray Quito's hit wasn't bad."

Daniel nodded in grim agreement.

* * *

Maggie really didn't know why she was bothering to volunteer at the hospital today. Her mind was consumed with Daniel, and every few minutes tears would build in her eyes and roll down her cheeks. Sick patients didn't need to be depressed even more by the sight of her glum face.

But she'd hoped that going to work—just as she always did on a Friday—would help her to feel more normal. Boy, was that a joke, she thought grimly. She was beginning to think her life would never be normal again. Not with this horrible ache in her heart.

Last night, when Daniel had called her, the mere sound of his voice had made her want to cave in, made her want to tell him she'd marry him tomorrow or the next day or anytime he wished. She'd come so close to doing just that, and she'd suddenly realized she couldn't keep their relationship just as occasional lovers. It was too deep for that. So she'd told him they shouldn't see each other anymore, that it would just be too painful for both of them.

Dear Lord, had she been right? she wondered. And what about all the pain she was feeling right now? Would it ever go away?

She was trying to blink away another set of tears when she caught the sight of flashing lights on the highway up ahead.

Slowing her car, she wiped her eyes with the back of her hand and peered at the vehicles that were blocking the road. It must be a car accident, she silently mused. There was an ambulance and several police cars parked at all angles on the highway.

When she came closer, a young officer held up his hand for her to stop and pull to the side of the road. She did as he requested, then rolled down her window as he approached the car.

"What's happened, Officer? Did someone have an accident?"

He shook his head, then glanced toward the commotion behind his shoulder as though he wasn't certain he should speak at all.

"There's been—you're going to have to wait, ma'am, maybe several minutes, before the road is cleared."

"Is someone hurt?" she asked, hoping it wasn't family or friends.

"Yes, ma'am," the officer said reluctantly. "There's been a shooting—"

He stopped in midsentence and hurried back to two more vehicles that had just driven up behind hers. Maggie used the opportunity to fling open the car door and jump quickly to the ground.

She could hear the officer desperately calling to her as she ran and stumbled toward the group of patrol cars. *Shooting. Ambulance. Lawmen. Daniel!*

Oh, God, please don't let it be him, she prayed as she wedged her way between two fenders and finally to the fringe of lawmen gathered around someone lying on a gurney.

The injured man was mostly hidden from

Maggie's view, making it impossible to guess his identity. But from the massive gathering of lawmen, she instinctively knew it was one of their own. As her eyes darted to each face in the crowd, her heart pounded painfully at her temples and in her ears until the telltale buzzing of an imminent fainting spell caused her to sway on her feet.

"Maggie! What the hell? What are you doing here?"

The sound of Daniel's voice jerked her back from the dark vortex she'd been about to fall into, and she looked dazedly around to see him striding up behind her.

Relief poured through her in such a swift, overwhelming way that her knees threatened to buckle. Thankfully, he grabbed her by the arm and steadied her.

"Daniel," she said in a hoarse whisper. "You're all right!"

"Of course I'm all right," he reassured her. "But why are you here?"

"I was going to work at the hospital. The road was blocked and one of the officers told me there'd been a shooting." She stared at him with eyes that were still dark with fear. "I thought—oh, God, I thought it was you!"

Unbearable horror washed over her and she yanked her arm away from him and hurried blindly toward her car. Daniel trotted after her.

"Maggie, stop! Wait!"

He grabbed her hand as she reached for door handle, but she shrugged his hand away and quickly slid into the driver's seat.

"No. I—can't handle this, Daniel. I can't handle us. Just leave me alone!"

Someone in the crowd yelled his name, and he looked impatiently from her to the group of lawmen.

"I gotta go," he said firmly. "But we're going to talk about this later, Maggie."

"No!" She pushed the button to raise the window, and she looked away from him as the glass separated their faces.

Finally he decided he couldn't spend any more time arguing with her and strode back to where they were loading the injured man in the ambulance.

Maggie started her car and maneuvered it back onto the highway. As she headed for home, her hands began to shake, and tears blinded her eyes.

It wasn't Daniel, this time, she thought with sick relief. But what about next time?

Chapter Twelve

A week later Daniel was sitting in a hard plastic chair, trying not to fall asleep as he listened to the beep, beep of the heart monitor next to the sheriff's hospital bed.

Daniel had left his office more than two hours ago and had been sitting here beside his boss ever since. It had only been three days since Quito had improved enough for the doctor to allow him to be moved out of the intensive care unit and into a private room.

Since that time, Daniel had hardly left the man's bed. The sheriff didn't have any family. Or at least, none that Daniel knew about. And since Quito had always been like an older brother to Daniel, he'd felt the need to be a brother back to Quito.

So far the sheriff had remained asleep and unresponsive to anyone's voice. Daniel had been praying hard to see some kind of sign that the sheriff hadn't suffered any brain damage from the shooting.

Restlessly he pushed himself out of the chair and went to the door of the room. Just outside in the hallway, another deputy stood guard.

"Seen anything unusual, Miguel?" Daniel asked the young man.

The deputy shook his head. "Nothing. But I won't let my guard down, Redwing. I don't care if it's the head of the hospital, he'll have to show me some ID before he gets in the sheriff's room."

"Good for you," Daniel said, patting his shoulder. "If you need to take a break, just let me know."

The deputy nodded to Daniel, who slipped back inside the hospital room. He walked over to Quito's bed and looked helplessly down at the sheriff's face. Oxygen was being pumped into his nose, and a bandage plastered the left side of his face where he'd been cut from flying glass. His usually dark skin was pale and clammy to the touch.

"Damn it, Quito, you've slept long enough," Daniel muttered. "And I'm getting sick of this hospital room. Wake up and talk to me!"

As usual there was no response from the man. With a heavy sigh, Daniel started around the bed to take up his position in the plastic chair. Halfway there he thought he heard a groan and he stopped in his tracks and stared at Quito's face.

His heart beating hopefully, he walked back to the sheriff's side and waited.

"Can you hear me, you sorry SOB?"

Quito's eyelids began to flutter and his lips worked. Daniel reached down and squeezed his arm.

"Redwing…is that you?"

The low, slurred question was like heaven to Daniel's ears, and he smiled broadly as Quito's eyes slowly opened.

Leaning his head closer to the other man's, he said, "Yes. It's me. Who'd you think it would be?"

"A blond angel with blue eyes."

"Sorry, buddy, I'm the only one who can put up with you for more than twenty-four hours."

"Yeah. That's true."

The sheriff lifted his hand and rubbed his nose. A frown marred his forehead as he felt the plastic hose running into both nostrils. "Damn! They got me on oxygen?"

"They've got you on everything, Quito. You nearly left us. But you're doing better now."

His expression fuzzy, he looked at Daniel. "I got shot. What did it do to me?"

"Shattered two ribs, blew a hole in your lung and collapsed it. They also had to take out your spleen. It was too mangled to save. You're lucky it wasn't your heart."

Quito closed his eyes and breathed deeply. "Hell, I don't have one of those. You know that."

Daniel knew just the opposite, but he played along with Quito's tough guy talk.

"Do you know who shot you?"

The sheriff's head moved back and forth upon the pillow. "A black pickup truck. Dodge, I think. Pulled up beside me—I thought the driver was just passing. The first shot shattered the window, but missed me. The second—I felt my side burning and then…I guess I passed out."

Daniel gave the man's arm another reassuring squeeze. "We're tracking down every lead, Quito. We'll find the bastard, I promise. All you need to do is get well."

"Yeah," he said weakly, then squinted up at Daniel. "And you need to go home and get some rest."

Daniel was about to object when the doctor suddenly entered the room. The tall young man was dressed in a white lab coat, a stethoscope dangling from around his neck. He was happy to see Quito was conscious and communicating. He asked the sheriff many questions before he finally reached for the clipboard attached to the end of the bed and began to scribble.

Daniel slipped from the room and waited outside with the guard until the doctor stepped into the hallway.

"How is he, Dr. Collins?" Daniel questioned the other man.

"Quito is improving. It's been slow going, but his regaining consciousness is a big step."

Daniel nodded with a measure of relief. "But you

do think he'll make a full recovery? He won't be permanently disabled from his injuries?"

Dr. Collins shook his head. "No. Other than the injuries he suffered, the sheriff is a strong, healthy man. I expect him to make a full recovery. Of course, we'll have to keep a close watch for infection and that sort of thing. And he'll have to spend several more days in the hospital. How many, I'm not sure yet. But rest assured he will recover."

"Thank you, Doctor. Thanks for everything."

The doctor nodded and walked across the hallway to catch an elevator. Once he disappeared, Daniel looked down at the guard and grinned.

"Did you hear that, Miguel? Quito is going to be okay!"

The young man's grin was as broad as Daniel's. "Yeah. Good news. Finally."

Daniel glanced at his watch. "I'm going to leave for a while, Miguel. Make sure you keep an eagle eye on who goes through this door. And if you feel sleepy at all, call the next deputy scheduled for guard duty. And if you need me for anything, you have my cell number. Right?"

"Right. Don't worry. Go on, you need to get out of here and rest," the young deputy assured him.

Feeling as though he could safely leave the hospital now that Quito was on the mend, Daniel caught the elevator and rode down to the bottom floor.

As he walked across the parking area to his truck, he punched in Jess's cell number. The second the undersheriff answered, Daniel said, "Quito's awake. The doctor says he's going to be okay."

Daniel could hear Jess let out a sigh of relief.

"Thank God for that. Did he remember anything about the shooting?"

"Not much. He couldn't see the person. A black pickup truck—a Dodge, he thinks, drove up beside him. Quito thought the truck was meaning to pass. Instead he fired into Quito's vehicle. The first shot shattered the window and missed Quito. He wasn't as lucky on the second one. After that, he says, he passed out. He doesn't remember."

Daniel climbed into his truck and started the engine. As he fastened his seat belt, Jess said, "Well, we know that when Leon Statler drove up on the scene, there was nothing but Quito's wrecked car with him inside and wounded. That was eight-fifteen. The suspect was probably long gone by the time Leon got to a phone and called 911 for help."

Leon, an old farmer who lived down the highway from Quito, had just happened to be going into town for chicken feed the morning of the shooting. If they were extremely lucky, the man might remember something about seeing a black truck.

"Maybe we ought to question Leon about the black truck. It might jog his memory," Daniel suggested.

"I'll question him," Jess told him. "You're officially off duty for the weekend. You need rest in the worst kind of way."

Daniel laughed mockingly. "And you don't?"

"I'll be fine. Uh, have you told Maggie about Quito?" Jess asked.

Daniel's jaw tightened. "No. She won't answer my calls."

"Give her time, Daniel. Women have to think everything through," Jess reasoned. "I'll tell her about Quito. That might help."

Daniel seriously doubted it, but he didn't bother to put his opinion in words. With Quito down, and the shooting investigation going full force, Jess had enough on his plate to deal with besides Daniel's personal life.

"If you're not going to let me work this weekend," Daniel told him, "I think I'll drive up to the reservation. My mother and grandfather haven't seen me in quite a while."

Going to his house and wandering around the quiet rooms was the last thing Daniel wanted to do. Everywhere he looked, he remembered Maggie being there, eating, sleeping, laughing and most of all, loving him. He couldn't sit around and dwell on her and remember and wish. He had to do something to make her see she was ruining something precious, and he could only hope his mother or grandfather had some words of wisdom to help him.

"Sounds good to me. Get gone and I'll see you when you get back," Jess told him.

Daniel thanked him, then clicked off the cell phone. Once he'd tossed the instrument onto the passenger seat, he quickly made a U-turn in the middle of the highway and headed toward Colorado.

Later that evening Daniel drove up to Pelipa Redwing's small, wood-framed house, located three miles west of Towaoc. Here the high-desert mountains stretched for miles, and the only living thing to see among the rock-strewn landscape was a sheep or a goat scavenging for a morsel of grass. But here the colors of the earth were unlike anywhere else Daniel had ever seen. Muted reds, yellows and purples streaked the mountains and made one think that heaven had to be near. But in reality Daniel knew the reservation was a harsh place to live.

"My son, is that you?"

His mother was standing in the open doorway, silhouetted by the light behind her. She appeared thin and frail, her shoulders bent just enough to add twenty years to her age. Each time Daniel saw her, he wanted to kill Robert Redwing all over again. But then, she hadn't been forced to love the man, he thought.

"Yes, it's me, Mother," he answered.

She waited until he reached the two rocks that served as steps before she reached out for him. He took her into his arms and for long moments said nothing as he held her close against him.

"It's late," she said after he'd finally released her. "Is something wrong?"

The sun had gone down an hour ago. That was late for a woman who lived on the desert with nothing more to do than feed her chickens and milk the goat.

"No. I just wanted to see you and Grandfather."

She smiled and took him by the arm. "Come in. You look so tired."

The house was no different from the way it had been when Daniel was a child. It was still sparsely decorated with linoleum covering the floors rather than carpet. He'd often offered to have the house carpeted for her so that the rooms would be warmer in the wintertime, but she always refused. A floor was meant to be swept, she often told him.

To his surprise and pleasure, he found his grandfather stretched out on a recliner in front of the television. Even though the screen was mostly snow, he seemed to be enjoying a rerun of *Bonanza.*

He went to greet the older man. "Grandfather, how are you?"

Joe SilverBear quickly turned off the television and rose to his feet. With both hands he clasped Daniel's hand and crushed it tightly.

The old Ute was tall and stick thin, with iron-gray braids and deeply creviced skin. Over the years his looks hadn't changed much, and Daniel wondered if Joe had always looked like an old man to him simply because he was his grandfather.

"It's good to see you, boy," Joe said. "Are you here for the night?"

Daniel nodded and glanced toward his mother. "I

hope you haven't thrown my things away. I didn't bring any clothes. I left from town."

She motioned for him to sit on the couch. "Everything is just like you left it," she said fondly. "You sit with your grandfather and I'll make coffee."

Daniel did as she suggested and Joe sank back into the recliner.

Once Pelipa was out of sight, Daniel turned a concerned eye on his grandfather. "Has Mother been ailing? Is that why you're here tonight?"

Normally at this time of night Joe would be at his own house, taking care of his dogs. He had a pen full of mongrels he believed should be treated like royalty. Apparently his grandfather had already taken care of the canines for the evening.

"No. Pelipa has been feeling okay." He waved his hand as though everything should be obvious to Daniel. "Your mother gets lonely, you know."

Daniel frowned as he crossed his legs out in front of him. "And why wouldn't she? This place is out in the middle of nowhere. She doesn't drive and she has only a handful of friends. She…no, both of you should come to Aztec and live. I could keep watch over both of you there."

Joe's lined face grew tight. "We don't belong there."

Daniel was about to argue when his mother appeared with a tray holding an old aluminum drip pot and three cups. Indian fry bread, dripping with honey, was piled on a nearby plate.

She served her father first, before she carried the tray over to Daniel. He poured himself a full cup of the coffee and took some of the fry bread. It was the first thing he'd eaten since early this morning.

"We heard about your sheriff," Pelipa said as she took a seat on the couch. "It was on the television news from Durango."

Daniel nodded and told them what he knew about the shooting and how Quito was getting along. The news obviously distressed his mother, and she looked at him with great concern.

"I worry the same thing will happen to you, Daniel. There's so much evil in the world today."

Pelipa Redwing didn't know the half of it, Daniel thought. Life here on the reservation might be harsh and limited but it was also sheltered. And for the first time since he'd contemplated the idea, Daniel realized this *was* the best place for his mother. She wasn't strong enough to see the seedy side of civilization.

"I could be hurt here on the reservation, Mother."

She nodded solemnly, and Daniel knew it would be her last word on the subject. To her, being submissive to her male relatives meant showing respect. But he'd often wished Pelipa would get riled and talk back, show the same sort of spunk and fight that Maggie did. At least she wasn't afraid to tell him how she felt about his work, even though she was afraid to marry him.

For the next hour Daniel finished off the coffee and fry bread while his mother and grandfather caught him up on local news. As usual most of the talk was about the revenue the new casino was bringing in and how they planned to build up the place. Daniel could plainly see that neither Pelipa nor Joe thought very highly of building up anything.

Finally, when the conversation dropped off, Daniel looked over at Joe SilverBear and said, "Grandfather, I've found the redheaded woman."

Daniel didn't have to say more. Joe remembered everything, especially his visions. The old man rose up in his chair and looked at Daniel with renewed interest.

"And have you asked her to marry you?"

Daniel nodded while Pelipa looked on with surprise.

"But she refuses," Daniel said starkly. "She's afraid that I will die—like her first husband. He was gored to death by a bull."

Pelipa's mouth dropped open with shock while Joe shook his head grimly.

"We never know what the Great Spirit holds in store for us," Joe said. "But there is a reason."

Daniel couldn't think of any reason why Maggie had suffered such a loss. But he didn't say this to his grandfather. Joe looked at most everything in a spiritual way and expected Daniel to do the same.

"Who is this woman, Daniel? How did you meet her?" his mother asked.

Even without the expression of surprise on Pelipa's face, Daniel knew the idea of her son wanting to marry was shocking for his mother. He'd often sworn to her that he would never marry or be caught up in the horrible situation that she'd been in with Robert Redwing. But then Maggie had come along with her softness and beauty and loving heart. And the world had suddenly changed for him.

"Her name is Maggie Ketchum and I met her through my work," Daniel answered. "She married into the rich Ketchum family that owns the T Bar K. They own thousands of acres of land and lots of horses and cattle."

"Then she is rich," Joe stated thoughtfully.

Pelipa frowned with confusion. "She doesn't sound like a person you would marry."

Daniel glanced back and forth between his mother and grandfather. They both looked hesitant and wary.

"Maggie doesn't live like she's rich. She's just a normal, down-to-earth woman. And she has a young son named Aaron. He's a good boy and we get along fine. He needs a father and I want to be that for him."

Joe began to nod, and Pelipa let out a long sigh.

"If this is the woman you want, then I'm glad you have found her," his mother said. "I've always prayed you would find someone, Daniel. Your heart is too good to stay empty the rest of your life."

Yet if Maggie wouldn't marry him, his heart *would* be empty the rest of his life, Daniel thought. If she refused to see him or even talk to him then his love would be a painful waste.

Rising from the couch, he gathered up his coffee cup

and the plate of bread crumbs. "If you two don't mind, I'm going to bed. I'll see you both in the morning."

Both Pelipa and Joe murmured their good-nights to him, and Daniel walked through the small house to the bedroom he'd used as a child.

His mother had never been one for change. Tonight as he looked around the small room he noticed that only the bedcover and the curtains at the windows were different. The plain pine bed was the same one he'd slept in as a small boy. The scarred chest of drawers had held what few clothes he'd owned.

There was a handful of pictures on the wall. All of them, except for one, were taken of him and Joe after a hunt or during a horseback ride through the rough cliffs and mountains of Mesa Verde. The last one, hanging a small distance away from the rest, was of Pelipa holding Daniel as a baby.

As Daniel unbuttoned his shirt, he walked over to the faded photo and peered into his mother's face. Even though she was standing on the same rock steps leading up to the front door of this very house, the photo seemed rather surreal to him. The camera shutter had caught Pelipa with a smile on her face and a light in her eye. Obviously, the moment in time had occurred before Robert Redwing had left his family and ruined Pelipa's life.

Doing his best to push that dour thought from his mind, Daniel switched off the light and finished undressing. The week had been long and harrowing. He was numb with fatigue and desperately needed sleep.

As his eyes adjusted to the darkness, he lay down on the narrow bed and turned his face toward the open window. Nights in the high desert were usually cool in summer, and the wind drifting through the open space carried the scent of sage across his pillow. The fragrance reminded him of Maggie and he fell asleep whispering her name.

The next morning Daniel slept past sunrise, something he hadn't done in years. Light was streaming through the window, warming his face and the sheet covering his body. He felt groggy and stiff. The realization hit him that he was in the same position he'd been in when he'd gone to sleep.

He could hear sounds of his mother moving around in the kitchen and smell the delicious odors of coffee, chorizo and eggs. For the first time in several days he felt hungry. He threw back the sheet and reached for his clothes.

After a quick wash, he found Pelipa in the kitchen, warming tortillas on an iron griddle. She was dressed in a tiered floral skirt with a long-sleeved shirt of a different pattern buttoned up to her neck. Her hair, which was mostly black with only a few gray streaks, was waist length, but she kept the wavy strands braided in a coronet on top of her head. Little birds, fashioned from turquoise stone, always hung from her earlobes, and a silver cuff bracelet circled her right wrist.

To Daniel she had always been a gentle, beautiful

woman. This was running through his mind as he went to her and kissed her cheek. "Good morning, Mother," he said, then glanced around. "Where's Grandfather?"

Pelipa carefully flipped one of the flour tortillas. "He's already had breakfast. He's gone to take care of his dogs."

"I'll go visit him later," Daniel said as he found himself a coffee cup and filled it from the drip pot on the gas stove. He'd bought his mother a modern coffeemaker last year thinking it would make the morning chore easier for her. The gift was still sitting in the closet, another example of her unwillingness to change.

While he sipped, Pelipa asked, "Did you sleep well, my son?"

"I don't think I even rolled over. I was very tired. The department has been working overtime since Quito was shot. Trying to find clues and track down leads. And then I drove every evening to Farmington to sit in his hospital room."

"I thought there was a hospital in Aztec," she said.

"There is," Daniel replied. "But the facilities aren't as well equipped to handle severe injures like Quito's."

Pelipa looked at him with gentle eyes. "Well, I'm glad he's better. But I'm sure it will be a long time before he can work again. You and Jess will have to take care of things, yes?"

Daniel smiled at her confidence in him. "Yes. And we will. Quito can rest easy on that."

She motioned for him to take a seat at the kitchen table, where she carried a plate filled with chorizo sausage and eggs and several warm tortillas.

Daniel dug hungrily into the food while his mother washed dishes at the sink. She was not one for many words, and he was finished with everything on his plate before she spoke again.

"Would you like to go help me gather the eggs?"

Gathering the eggs was a woman's chore and something she normally wouldn't ask Daniel to do. But he was happy that she seemed to want him along today, he thought as he rose from his chair and carried his dishes to the sink.

"I'd be glad to. It's been a long time since I saw the inside of the henhouse."

She collected a large basket from the pantry, and the two of them walked out a door leading to the backyard. From this side of the house, the ground was mainly flat and swept several miles into the distance before rock buttes jutted from the earth like sentinels guarding its native people. Closer to the house, the ground was rocky and mostly barren. Purple sage and clumps of wiry grass grew in tufts here and there. In a few spots prickly choya bloomed bright pink and yellow.

Daniel supposed the area held its own rough beauty, but he'd often wished better for his mother. He'd even pleaded with her to move to Aztec, where she could have a yard with grass and gentle flowers without thorns in the summer. But this was where

Pelipa felt comfortable and at home, so he didn't push the issue.

The henhouse was some thirty yards behind the house. It was built with a combination of old lumber and corrugated iron. Chicken wire surrounded the front of the structure and stretched several feet outward to make a yard for the hens to roam in without the chance of them being eaten by a coyote.

Daniel opened the gate to the chicken yard and followed his mother inside. Several Domineckers and Rhode Island Reds were pecking at corn chips that Pelipa had scattered on the ground for them to eat.

Daniel said, "You've gotten more hens since I was last here. Did you hatch some yourself?"

"No. Your grandfather brought the Reds back from Cortez. I didn't need them but he likes the nice big eggs. I'm thinking about letting one of the Domineckers set. Meda has been hinting that she'd like two or three."

Meda was a distant cousin who lived in Towaoc. Since the old woman didn't drive and had no other family to speak of, Joe often drove her and Pelipa together to the grocery store and to do other necessary errands.

Daniel said, "She doesn't have a henhouse. Where would she keep them?"

"Probably on the porch. You remember, son, her mother, Josie, was from the southern tribe. And she never was very civilized."

Daniel wanted to throw back his head and howl

with laughter, but he couldn't. Not when his mother was deadly serious.

Instead he said, "Well, maybe once you get the chicks, Grandfather will be civilized enough to make her some coops to keep them in."

They went inside the little barn where several hens' nests, made of hay packed in wooden crates, lined the walls.

Pelipa handed Daniel the basket, then went to the first nest. "I wanted you to come out here with me so that I could talk to you," she said as she dug a brown egg from under the hay.

Daniel wondered what was wrong with talking inside the house, but he didn't voice the question out loud. Like his grandfather, Pelipa had her reasons for doing things, and he'd been taught not to question their actions. They were his elders and his family, and he was to learn from them, not the other way around.

"Okay," he said.

Pelipa went to the next nest and plucked up two more eggs. "Do you love this Maggie Ketchum?"

As he watched his fragile mother move from one nest to the next, he figured she had lain awake most of the night thinking about him and his wish to marry. It wasn't surprising that she wanted to question him on the subject this morning.

"More than my own breath."

His mother turned and studied him for long, quiet moments and then she moved across the dirt floor to where he stood. After she placed the brown eggs in the basket, she lifted her hands and cupped them around his face.

"Then you must go to her and tell her so."

Daniel's heart squeezed with pain. "I've already told her, Mother. She's afraid of losing me."

She gently patted both his cheeks before she dropped her hands to her sides. "I know what it's like to lose a man. I understand what she's gone through. It's not something I would ever want to go through again. That's why—"

Pelipa stopped and looked away from him as though just talking about her husband shamed her.

"That's why you've never remarried," he finished for her.

She nodded and Daniel sighed.

"I am not like Robert Redwing," he said firmly. "I would never, by choice, leave my wife or child."

Her expression solemn, Pelipa nodded again. "I am certain of that, too."

Daniel helplessly threw up his hands. "Then how am I going to make Maggie understand this?"

"Go to her. Stand by her side no matter what. That's where your father failed. When I needed him the most, he wasn't strong enough to stand beside me."

Daniel wanted to shout with frustration. This last week without Maggie had been pure hell for him. His mind was constantly jammed with solutions to reason with her fear. So far he'd come up with none. He couldn't even get the woman to talk to him!

"And how can I do that if she won't let me?" he asked his mother.

A faint smile lifted the corners of Pelipa's mouth. "If she loves you, she will let you."

His mother made it sound so simple and easy. And maybe it was, he thought, with a sudden spark of hope. Maybe staying away from the T Bar K and not forcing her to speak with him was giving Maggie the wrong impression about his commitment to her. If she saw that he wasn't going to back down or give up on her, she might take a second look at their situation.

Bending his head, he placed a kiss on Pelipa's forehead. "Thank you, Mother, for understanding. I'll try again with Maggie, and keep trying until I can convince her."

"Good."

A wistful smile crossed his face. "And now that we are on the subject, don't you think it's time that you put the past behind you and found yourself a companion?"

She looked at him in shocked wonder. "Daniel, you know that I'm too old for such things!"

"You're not old, Mother. The heart is never too old to love. Maggie has taught me that much."

Uncertainty flickered in her eyes, and then she stared down at the basket and the eggs nestled among the straw. "I'll think about that, Daniel. I'll think about it really hard."

Hope surged inside him, and he gathered his mother close to his chest and hugged her tight.

Chapter Thirteen

Later that afternoon on the T Bar K, Maggie was breathing a sigh of relief as she talked on the telephone to Victoria.

"The doctor says Quito is steadily improving. Jess thinks he might even get out of the hospital by the end of next week."

"I'm so glad to hear this news," Maggie said to her sister-in-law. "That morning when I drove up on the scene—" She stopped and shuddered as the memory of the overwhelming fear she'd experienced washed over her. When she'd spotted Daniel, alive and well, something inside her had snapped. She'd been angry. Angry because she'd been so afraid, and angry because he'd put her in such a situation in the first place. "Well...I'm just glad Quito's going to recover."

"Jess says Daniel is wearing himself out driving over to Farmington every evening to sit with him. For the first two nights after the accident, Daniel didn't even leave the hospital. Jess ordered him to go home and get some sleep, but Daniel refused. You know, Quito doesn't have any family. None that we know of, and I guess Daniel wants to be there for him."

Yes, Daniel would be that way, Maggie thought wistfully. He was a good man with a good heart. She could look to the ends of the earth and never find one that she could love more. So why couldn't she be brave enough to tell him she would be his wife?

"He's very close to Quito," was all that Maggie could manage to say.

Victoria didn't reply for several moments, and Maggie was about to ask her if she was still there when the other woman asked, "How are things with you and Daniel?"

The question had Maggie staring numbly at the living room wall. These past few days she'd never missed anyone as much as she'd missed Daniel. It was killing her to stay away from him, to avoid the telephone when his number lit up on Caller ID. She honestly didn't know how much more she could go on before she began to break apart.

"Not good."

"Why?"

"Victoria! I've told you why. The man is a deputy! He could wind up shot just like Sheriff Perez. Only, he might not be so lucky as Quito. It might kill him! I can't deal with that kind of uncertainty."

Victoria huffed out an impatient breath. "Jess was shot and nearly killed, too. But I didn't run off wringing my hands. Just ask yourself, Maggie, do you want to live your life alone and miserable? Would that be better?"

Dropping her head, Maggie massaged the deep furrows in her forehead. "I...just don't know anymore, Victoria. I desperately want to see him, but I think that would only make things worse and..."

She paused as Aaron ran into the room and spotted her talking on the telephone. In an instant he was standing at the side of her chair, shaking her arm for attention.

"Uh, excuse me, Victoria. Aaron just came in. I'll talk to you later."

Scowling at her son, she placed the receiver back on its hook. "Why were you interrupting my conversation?" she demanded. "I've told you never to do that unless it was an emergency."

The boy pushed out his lower lip. "Well, it *was* an emergency. I wanted to know if you were talking to Daniel."

Maggie let out an inward sigh. For several days now, Aaron had been listening for the phone and watching the road, expecting Daniel to call or show up in the front driveway. And every day that passed without a word from Daniel, she could see her son growing gloomier and gloomier.

"No," she said to him. "I was talking to your aunt Victoria."

Crestfallen, he muttered, "Oh. I was hoping it was him. Today is Saturday, and he doesn't work on Saturday. He might come over if you'd call him."

Maggie rose from the chair and began to gather up a clutter of dirty dishes and papers from the coffee table. "No. We've been through this before, Aaron. Daniel and I...well, we have some problems to work out."

Aaron jammed his hands on his hips as he glared angrily at his mother. "Why won't you talk to him? It's your fault that he won't come see me! You've told him to stay away. You don't care that I love him and want him to be my father!"

Maggie was incredulous at Aaron's outburst, and she straightened up from the coffee table to stare at her son.

"Aaron! You have a father!" She walked over to the fireplace mantel and plucked down a picture of Hugh. Pointing toward the glass, she said, "This was—is your father!"

Aaron strode over to her, and Maggie's heart nearly broke as she spotted the tears in his eyes and the quiver of his compressed lips.

"I'm not a little baby, Mom. I'm old enough to understand that Hugh Ketchum was my real dad. But he's not here anymore. He can't talk to me or do things with me. Just looking at his picture doesn't make up for any of that."

Her first instinct was to scold him again for not showing more respect, but the words died quickly on her tongue. She hadn't been the only person to suffer because of Hugh's death. Aaron had suffered, too, and because of her fear of the future, she was continuing to make her son pay the price.

Placing her arm around his shoulders, she gently pulled him to her side and hugged him tightly. "Aaron, I'm sorry. I should have been listening to you. I should have been thinking about your wants instead of just mine. Will you forgive me?"

He looked up at her and blinked back the tears. "Will you call Daniel?"

She nodded slowly. "But don't expect him to race right over here to see you. He has work and lots of other things to do."

And he might not ever want to speak to her again, Maggie thought sickly. And she could hardly blame him. So many times he'd tried to reach out to her, and she'd done nothing but push him away.

Maggie walked over to the phone and punched in Daniel's number while Aaron danced around on his toes and rubbed his hands together with glee. But his joy was short-lived when she hung up the phone without speaking.

"What's the matter? Didn't he answer?" Aaron questioned.

Maggie shook her head. "I reached his answering

machine. He's out of town and won't be back until later this evening."

"Oh. Well, I guess we'll just have to wait," he mumbled.

Unable to stand the sight of her son being so dejected, Maggie suddenly suggested, "Okay. What do you say the two of us walk down to the ranch yard and take a long ride on a couple of horses from the remuda? By the time we get finished with the ride, Daniel might be home."

It wasn't often that Maggie rode horseback with her son, so the unexpected gesture pleased him immensely and he flung his arms around her waist. "Yeah! Thanks, Mom!"

The drive from Towaoc to Aztec had never seemed longer to Daniel. On several of the long, straight stretches across the desert, he'd pretty much floored his truck and broken all sorts of speed limits. It was good he hadn't met a highway patrol. Daniel wasn't sure how he would have explained his reckless driving. No officer of the law wanted to hear lovesickness as an excuse for speeding.

But now that he'd talked to his mother, he was more than just anxious to see Maggie. He felt determined and even more certain that the two of them were meant to be together. Now all he had to do was convince her of that.

The winding mountain road to the T Bar K was rough and rocky, and once he started the climb to the ranch yard, Daniel had to slow his speed greatly. He was creeping past the barns and feed lots, heading up the mountain to Maggie's house, when the corner of his left eye suddenly caught a flash of red and brown colors moving rapidly.

Slowing the truck, he looked over toward the ranch yard and spotted a commotion in one of the dusty lots. A horse was bucking wildly, sending plumes of red dust rising into the air. The other horses tied nearby to a long hitching post were breaking loose in fear and racing around the lot, searching for a place to flee the uproar.

Daniel stopped the truck, rolled down the glass and squinted for a closer look. The rider was still in the saddle, but the way the horse was bucking he doubted a professional bronc rider could stay glued for much longer.

And then he spotted Aaron to one side of it all. He appeared to be screaming as he frantically waved his arms at the rider.

Dear God, the boy was going to be run over or hit by a flying hoof!

Daniel stomped on the gas and directed the truck straight for the horse lot. After bouncing wildly over a deep ditch and several boulders, he finally skidded the truck to stop, then jumped onto the fence.

Aaron spotted him and shouted desperately. "Daniel! Daniel! It's Mom! She's gonna fall off!"

At that moment Daniel looked over to see the figure on the back of the bucking horse sail through the air like a rag doll. The felt hat on the rider's head flew off, and Daniel was stunned to see a flash of Maggie's red curls just before she landed with a hard thump on the rocky ground.

Terrified now, he jumped over the corral fence and raced over to her motionless body. Behind him, he could hear some of the ranch hands racing up to see what was happening. Aaron was right behind him, too, and the boy stood white-faced at his mother's feet while Daniel squatted down at her head.

"Maggie!" he cried. "Maggie!"

Her face was in the dirt and Daniel gently rolled her over and brushed the red curls off her cheeks. She sputtered and her eyelids began to flutter.

"Maggie, can you hear me?"

"She's gonna wake up. She's *gotta* wake up," Aaron said in hushed fear.

"She'll be all right, son. Don't you worry, now."

This was from the old ranch hand, Skinny, while the rest of the men also murmured assurances to the boy.

Daniel scarcely heard anything they were saying as he gently cradled Maggie's head on his knee. Dear God, please let her be okay, he desperately prayed.

"Give me some water!" he shouted the order to no one in particular. "There's a canteen in my truck!"

One of the cowboys quickly fetched the insulated container and handed it down to Daniel. He ripped a white handkerchief from the back pocket of his jeans and soaked the soft fabric with the cool water before he wiped it across her forehead.

In a matter of moments her eyelids fluttered again, then opened completely. Her gaze focused immediately on Daniel's face and she frowned, bewildered.

"Da-Daniel? Is that...you?"

The questions were mumbled around gasps for air, but they were enough to put a smile of relief on Daniel's face and he leaned down and kissed her dusty cheek. "Yes, it's me. Do you know what happened?"

Shifting, Maggie tried to push herself to a sitting position. Daniel quickly slipped his arm beneath her shoulder and propped her back against his knee. She breathed deeply as she tried to regain the air that had been knocked from her lungs.

"Yes, I remember. Rooster bucked me off!" She looked up and scanned the crowd of men until her gaze settled on a young man with wavy blond hair and a handlebar mustache. "It was your mare, Joel!" she said accusingly. "As I was riding into the lot, she kicked Rooster in the side with both hind feet and he was pretty unhappy about it!"

"Sorry, ma'am. She gets a bit temperamental at times."

Maggie rolled her eyes, and a rumble of chuckles passed through the men. Aaron went down on his knees and hugged his mother close.

"Are you okay, Mom?"

She reached up to hug him and immediately

groaned with pain. "Oh honey…yes. But my wrist! I think it might be broken!"

Aaron eased back, and Daniel lifted the injured limb for a closer inspection.

"It looks crooked," he stated gravely. "Can you move your fingers?"

She attempted his request and cried out again. "No! Oh, it hurts, Daniel."

He looked up at the cowboy with the guilty mare. "Get my truck and drive it in here. I'm going to take her to the hospital."

"And get these damned horses tied up and out of the way, boys!" Skinny began to shout. "This ain't no party we're havin' around here."

On the way to the hospital, Maggie had Daniel use his cell phone to call Victoria. The doctor met them at the emergency room and managed to cut through some of the red tape so that they could get Maggie X-rayed more quickly.

While Daniel and Maggie waited in an examining room for the X-rays to be read, Victoria announced she was going to take Aaron to the cafeteria for a snack.

As the two of them started out the door, Victoria tried to assure Maggie. "The painkiller they gave you will start working soon. Just sit there and try to relax until the doctor gets here."

"What if I need a cast?" Maggie asked worriedly. "Will you do that for me?"

Victoria shot her a good-natured frown. "No. We'll let the bone doctor take care of you. And will you quit being such a worrywart? Aaron was a much better patient when he had his tonsils removed. Take care of her, Daniel," Victoria said over her shoulder. "She can be a handful at times."

Aunt and nephew left the room, and from a plastic chair in the corner Daniel looked at Maggie. She was sitting on the edge of the examining table with her injured wrist lying limply in her lap. Dirt was smeared on her jeans and shirt and her hair was covered with dust.

Maggie turned her gaze on him and raised her brows in anticipation of a scolding. Even though the cow-bred quarter horses used on the ranch were mainly well broken, they weren't as predictable as her own personal mount. But she'd been so down all week and she'd wanted to give Aaron and herself a different treat.

"You know," Daniel said. "There for a while you were giving Rooster one hell of a ride. I don't think I'd have lasted that long."

The compliment was the last thing she expected to hear from him and she began to laugh.

The free, easy sound brought Daniel to his feet and he moved around the table so that he was standing directly in front of her.

"It's good to hear you laugh," he said.

Her heart throbbed with uncertainty as she searched his eyes with hers. "It's good that I have you here to make me laugh," she said.

"Maggie, I—"

"I tried to—"

They both spoke at once and then fell silent. Maggie reached out for his hand. He took it as he leaned forward and pressed his cheek against hers.

"Oh, God, Maggie, I was so scared when I saw you go flying off that horse. You could have broken your neck! You could have been killed!"

She could feel his fear vibrating through his fingertips and in his voice. And in that instant she knew that she had been looking at everything so stupidly, so selfishly.

"I know, Daniel," she said with a rueful groan. "Forgive me. Not just for giving you a fright. But for being so blind about you…about us. Now I can see—I realize—that losing a spouse can work both ways. You don't have any guarantees that I'll be around until we grow old. Just like I don't have a guarantee that you will."

Curling his arms around her, he held her against him and kissed her softly. "I spent the night with my mother and grandfather last night and I told them about you. About how I want to marry you."

Joy spread through her and chased away every doubtful shadow lingering inside her. "What did they think? Are they disappointed that I'm not a Ute?"

Daniel shook his head. "My mother was surprised and happy. And you know what, Maggie? For the first time in my life, I believe I understand a little of why she married my father. She loved him. She couldn't help herself. The heart has a way of leading us, even if it sometimes isn't in the right direction."

She tilted her head back to gaze upon his face. "But we're in the right direction, Daniel. That morning I came up on the site where Quito was shot, all I could think about was facing the future without you. Now—I'm just thankful it wasn't you. I can see that each day of our life is meant to be cherished. Whether those days are many or few, I need you in them with me."

"Maggie. My Maggie," he whispered softly as his fingers stroked her cheek. "We'll always be together. And each spring we'll have our own bear dance, we'll leave a plume on the cedar, and we'll start afresh…with each other."

Tears of blissful joy slipped from the corners of her eyes, and he kissed each one away as it trailed down her dusty cheeks.

"I love you, Daniel Redwing. So much. So much."

"We're getting married next week," he said firmly. "It doesn't matter to me where or how we get it done. I'll leave that up to you. Just so we become man and wife."

Rearing her head back, she looked at him with surprise. "Next week? But, Daniel, I might have to wear a cast on my wrist for several weeks! Am I going to walk down the aisle like that?"

He gave her a sexy, lopsided grin. "I won't be looking at the cast. I'll be looking at my beautiful wife."

She was making a move to kiss him when an elderly doctor with white hair suddenly walked through the door with a young nurse close on his heels. The doctor introduced himself, and Daniel quickly stepped out of the way so the physician could attend to his patient.

After giving her crooked wrist a cursory glance, he patted her knee and said, "Well, Ms. Ketchum, I can safely say that you have two breaks in your wrist. But thankfully they're clean breaks and no tendons were torn. You won't need surgery but you will need to wear a cast for about six weeks."

Maggie looked at Daniel and rolled her eyes. He merely smiled and winked at her.

"I'm glad it wasn't worse," she told the doctor. "I'll wear the cast for as long as I need to."

The doctor gave her another reassuring smile. "Good. Nurse Bradley will be putting that on for you in a few minutes and then I'll sign a release so that you can go home."

"What about the rest of her, Doctor?" Daniel asked. "She took a very hard fall. Could there be anything else wrong with her?"

The kindly doctor peered more closely at his patient. "It's possible. That's why I want to give her a full exam." He made a motion for Daniel to leave the room. "There's a waiting area just down the hall. Someone will let you know when we're finished with her."

Daniel was being dismissed, and there was nothing he could do about it, so he left Maggie with the capable doctor and found a seat in a waiting room that was empty. In one corner a television was tuned in to the Weather Channel. He stared at the geological maps marked with suns and rain clouds while he hoped and prayed that Maggie hadn't sustained any other hidden injuries.

After a few minutes, Victoria and Aaron returned from the cafeteria, and the two of them sat beside him to wait. An hour and then some passed before a nurse finally appeared pushing Maggie in a wheelchair.

The first thing Daniel noticed was that her face was much whiter and she looked slightly dazed. Fear sliced through him but he did his best to keep it from his face as the three of them hurried to meet her.

"What's wrong?" he asked without preamble.

"Are you going to live?" Victoria teased.

Maggie gave them a hesitant smile and then her gaze settled softly on Daniel's face.

"Uh, Victoria would you take Aaron out to the truck? I…I'd like to talk to Daniel alone for a minute or two."

"Sure. Take your time," Victoria said, and curled her arm around her nephew's shoulders. "Come on, buddy, let's go count the stars while we wait for these two."

Maggie expected Aaron to put up a fuss, but he surprised her by leaving eagerly with his aunt, and she breathed a sigh of relief.

Daniel assured the nurse that he could push Maggie safely outside to the curb, and though she appeared reluctant to give him free rein over the wheelchair, she wasn't about to argue with the chief deputy of San Juan County.

"I didn't need this thing," Maggie said moments later as he stopped the chair in a small foyer and helped her to her feet. "But it's mandatory that a patient leave in one."

"I'm not so sure that you should walk on your own," Daniel said with concern. "You look worse now than when we first came in. Is your wrist hurting more?"

She smiled at him, and he could see her lips were quivering and there was a strange sort of light in her eyes that caused his heart to beat with uncertainty.

"No," she answered. "It's much better. I hardly feel anything at all."

"Then something else is the matter. Why didn't the doctor put you in a hospital room? What is it? Broken ribs? A concussion? I..."

Stepping close to him, she placed her palms on his chest and looked up at him. "The doctor says I'm going to have a baby."

Stunned, he grabbed her shoulders and stared at her. "A baby! But we—it's only been a short time since we—how could he know?" he finally managed to sputter the question.

"The doctor was about to write me a prescription for painkillers, and he asked if there was any chance I might be pregnant. I had to tell him yes, so he ran a quick blood test. They have those now that can detect if a woman is only a few days pregnant. I am."

Incredible joy swept over Daniel's face, and he grabbed her around the waist and lifted her off her feet. Giggling, she wrapped her arms around him and lifted her lips to his.

He kissed her for long, long moments, until someone entering the double-door entrance finally interrupted them, and Daniel carefully set her back on her feet.

"A baby," he whispered incredibly. "Maggie, you've made me the happiest man alive!"

The joy on her face sobered for a moment. "Are you really, Daniel? Please be honest with me. Maybe you're wishing this could have happened later."

He frowned with amazement. "Later? Honey, I don't want anything we do to be 'later.' We have a lot of living to do, starting now, this very moment."

She let out a long sigh of relief and pressed her cheek against his chest. "You know, I think that night we camped out and made love without any protection...I think we were both trying to say I love you."

And he'd been saying it in his mind and his heart ever since, Daniel thought. "Thank God Aaron likes to fish," he mused aloud.

Maggie laughed softly and clasped her hand around his. "Come on. Let's go tell Aaron he's going to get what he wished for."

Daniel glanced at her as the two of them left the building. "Oh? What's that? A brother or sister?"

She laughed again, and Daniel realized he was going to enjoy that sound for the rest of his life.

"No. We'll tell him about that later—after the

wedding. His wish was to have you as his father. Think you're going to like being called Daddy?"

He squeezed her hand as he looked up and saw Aaron running toward them.

"I wouldn't have it any other way."

* * * * *

If you enjoy the
MEN OF THE WEST *series,*
don't miss the next book,
From Here to Texas
by Stella Bagwell,
out in September 2006.

0706/23b

SPECIAL EDITION™

THEIR UNEXPECTED FAMILY
by Judy Duarte

Montana

Pregnant Juliet Rivera was finally taking a rest, and reporter Mark Anderson was taking an interest in her. But would Mark ever be able to put his demons to rest and find love with the beautiful mother-to-be?

THE RIGHT MAN? by Arlene James

Lucky in Love

Sierra Carlson had inherited money and brawny young farmer Sam Jayce had come up with the perfect business plan—one that meshed her career dreams with his. But working so closely with Sam inspired dreams of a very different sort!

SHE'S HAVING A BABY
by Marie Ferrarella

The Cameo

When MacKenzie Ryan was given a necklace that was meant to find her true love, she was cynical—she was heartbroken and…pregnant! But her scepticism gave way with the arrival of a handsome, sexy new neighbour, Quade Preston…

Don't miss out!

On sale from 21st July 2006

Available at WHSmith, Tesco, ASDA, Borders, Eason, Sainsbury's and most bookshops

www.silhouette.co.uk